"You're beautiful."

Startled, Audrey whipped around to find herself staring into the dark eyes of John Doe. His lopsided grin sucked the breath from her lungs. She'd never understood the term *roguishly handsome* until this moment. Even groggy and on pain meds, he affected her on an elemental level. Which made her extremely uneasy. What would he be like fully conscious?

Heart pounding, she stepped closer to the bed. "Who are you? What's your name?"

His eyelids fluttered, and he said something unintelligible.

She reached for the button to call the nurse when his fingers closed over her wrist, pressing against her skin where the sleeve of her uniform rode up. Strong hands, and calloused, she noted in a bemused way that made her twitchy.

"You look like a Christmas ornament." His words were slurred. "Shiny. Pretty."

His hand dropped away as if he could no longer hold on. His head lolled to the side and his eyes closed.

"Hey," Audrey sai̶d ̶ ̶ ̶ ̶ ̶ ̶ ̶ "Mister, I need you to wak̶

But he'd gone ou̶

Terri Reed's romance and romantic suspense novels have appeared on the *Publishers Weekly* top twenty-five and Nielsen BookScan's top one hundred lists, and have been featured in *USA TODAY, Christian Fiction Magazine* and *RT Book Reviews*. Her books have been finalists for the Romance Writers of America RiTA® Award, the National Readers' Choice Award and three times for the American Christian Fiction Writers Carol Award. Contact Terri at terrireed.com or PO Box 19555, Portland, OR 97224.

Visit the Author Profile page at Harlequin.com for more titles.

IDENTITY UNKNOWN

TERRI REED

⟨H⟩ **HARLEQUIN**® LOVE INSPIRED® SUSPENSE

Recycling programs
for this product may
not exist in your area.

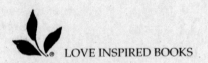

LOVE INSPIRED BOOKS

ISBN-13: 978-0-373-44770-1

Identity Unknown

www.Harlequin.com

Printed in U.S.A.

Have I not commanded you? Be strong and courageous. Do not be afraid; do not be discouraged, for the Lord your God will be with you wherever you go.
–Joshua 1:9

To my family for always believing in me
and to Leah for friendship and laughter.

ONE

"Two guards at the south entrance." Canada Border Services Agency officer Nathanial Longhorn spoke into the microphone attached to his flak vest.

On the cold December morning, Nathanial stared through the scope on his C7 assault sniper rifle from his perch on the southeast corner of a warehouse overlooking the commercial shipping port of Saint John Harbour, New Brunswick. The overcast sky shadowed the world in a gray haze.

His breath condensed into a white cloud, obscuring his vision in the threatening chill of an impending snowstorm. A whiteout was the last thing his team needed. He prayed the bad weather held off for a few more hours.

"Copy that." Through Nathanial's earpiece came the reply from his friend and fellow Integrated Border Enforcement Taskforce team member, US Immigration and Customs Enforcement agent Blake Fallon.

Blake motioned and two members of the team below split off to subdue the guards.

Nathanial kept an alert eye for anything that would impede or jeopardize the IBETs members on the ground as they stealthily made their way down the street to another warehouse a block away.

They were determined to bring down an arms dealer and his network of smugglers who illegally brought small and large weapons across the border between the two countries. The latest intelligence reported a shipment of handguns would be brought into Canada tonight.

The men who made up the IBETs team were from various law enforcement agencies on both sides of the international boundary line between Canada and the United States. Nathanial was proud to be a part of the team and would give his life for each and every one of the other team members regardless of their nationality.

The successful completion of this mission would be a welcome Christmas present, indeed.

He intended to head home to Saskatchewan for a much-needed respite with his family. Though he doubted the visit would be very relaxing. His mother and grandmother would be on him about fulfilling his destiny and settling down to provide grandchildren.

An old sorrow stirred, but he quickly tamped it down.

Despite his grandmother's certainty that there was a soul mate out there for him, Nathanial was skeptical about love and marriage. He'd come close once with his high school sweetheart, but that relationship had ended in tragedy and heartbreak. He'd decided then going it alone was better than opening himself up to that kind of pain again.

Besides, he liked his bachelor life too much to tie the knot like some of his friends and coworkers. Though Nathanial never lacked for female company, the thought of hearth and home made him want to run screaming into the night.

Being domesticated wasn't on his agenda. He was over thirty and set in his ways. He liked the freedom of taking off on an assignment at a moment's notice. He enjoyed the variety of dating different women, always careful to make sure any woman he spent time with knew he wasn't interested in anything serious or long-term.

Some ladies took that as a challenge to change his mind, and others walked away before they became too attached.

He tolerated the former until he couldn't and appreciated the latter.

He'd yet to meet a woman who made him want to change his mind. And frankly, he doubted he ever would.

A chill skated over the nape of his neck, drawing his attention to the current assignment. Once the two guards were out of commission, Nathanial did another visual sweep. All appeared clear. Good. He was cold and ready to wrap this up so he could have a cup of hot coffee and warm himself by a roaring fire.

He was about to give the go-ahead to the team when his attention snagged on a gold luxury sedan turning onto the street a few blocks away.

The arms dealer? Or someone in the wrong place at the wrong time? "Hold up."

He prayed the car kept driving, because if it didn't, this op was going to become more complicated.

Behind him, the scuff of a shoe on the concrete roof sent his heart hammering. He rolled onto his back, bringing the rifle up, his finger hovering over the trigger. A man loomed over him. Confusion and panic vied for dominance. Then the butt of an automatic submachine gun rammed into his skull.

And the world went dark.

Deputy Sheriff Audrey Martin sang along with the Christmas carol playing on the patrol car radio. The first fingers of dawn rose over the horizon. From her spot parked on a rise overlooking the small fishing village she'd been born in, she surveyed the streets and buildings of the township of Calico Bay, Maine, dusted in white.

This early-morning patrol was her favorite time, especially in winter. Gone were the summer windjammers and tour boats from the harbor. Now only the commercial fishing vessels and tugboats remained, most of which were already out to sea, while everyone else stayed snug in their beds. The population of the town receded to those whose lives began and ended here. Fishermen who made their living off the ocean, always hunting for a good day's catch, and those who supported the fishing industry.

She'd been on the job for less than a year and already she wanted to run for sheriff when the office's current occupant retired. There would be those who would cry nepotism, because Sheriff David Crump was her mother's aunt's husband. And there would be those who would oppose her for the simple fact she was female. Two strikes against her.

But she'd win them over with her capabilities. She had to. Failure wasn't an option. Too many people expected her to fail. She wanted to disappoint them. She wanted to make her family proud. Especially her mother and father, rest his soul.

He'd been gone since she was a child, but she still wanted to honor his memory by doing well and serving her community.

Having grown up with a doctor for a mother and a fisherman for a father, she knew hard work and commitment were the keys to succeeding. Not that she needed much beyond her studio apartment and the respect of the town.

Though her mother constantly warned her if she didn't take another chance on love, she'd end up old and alone.

Better that than having her heart trampled on all over again. Those were three years of her life she'd never get back. Three years wasted on a man who had cheated on her and then called her a fool for believing in love.

Well, she wouldn't be making that mistake again.

She warmed her hands in front of the car's heater vents and sang beneath her breath, not really in tune but enjoying singing anyway. Outside the confines of the patrol car, snow flurries swirled in the gray morning light and danced on the waves of the Atlantic Ocean crashing on the shores of Calico Bay, a sweeping inlet that formed a perfect half-moon with a picturesque view of their friends across the waterway in New Brunswick.

The radio attached to her uniform jacket crackled and buzzed before the sheriff's department dispatcher, Ophelia Leighton, came on the line. "Unit one, do you copy?"

Thumbing the answer button, Audrey replied, "Yes, dispatch, I copy."

"Uh, there's a reported sighting of a—"

The radio crackled and popped. In the background, Audrey heard Ophelia talking, then the deep timbre of the sheriff's voice. "Uh, sorry about that." Ophelia came back on the line. "We're getting mixed reports, but bottom line there's something washed up on the shore of the Pine Street beach."

"Something?" Audrey buckled her seat belt, shifted the car into Drive and took off toward the north side of town. "What kind of something?"

"Well, one report said a beached whale," Ophelia came back with. "Another said dead shark. But a couple people called in to say a drowned fisherman."

Audrey's gut clenched. All sorts of things found their way into the inlet from the ocean's current. None of those scenarios sounded good. Especially the last one. The town didn't need the heartache of losing one of their own so close to Christmas. Not that any time was a good time.

Her heart cramped with sorrow for the father she'd lost so many years ago to the sea.

She prayed that whoever was on the beach wasn't someone she knew. It would be sad enough for a stranger to die on their shore.

Pine Street ended at a public beach, which in the summer would be teeming with tourists and locals alike. She brought her vehicle to a halt in the cul-de-sac next to an early-model pickup truck where a small group of gawkers stood on the road side of the concrete barrier. Obviously the ones who'd called the sheriff's department.

Bracing herself for the biting cold, she climbed out and plopped her brimmed hat on her head to prevent her body heat from escaping through her scalp. With shoulders squared and head up, she approached the break in the seawall.

"Audrey." Clem Previs rushed forward to grip her sleeve, his veined hand nearly blue from the cold. The retired fisherman ran the bait shop on the pier with his two sons. "Shouldn't you wait for the sheriff?"

Others crowded around her. Mary Fleischer from the dime store. Pat Garvey from the hardware store and the librarian, Lucy Concord. All stared at her with expectant and skeptical gazes. These men and women had watched her grow up from a wee babe to the woman she was today. She held affection for each one, and their lack of confidence in her hurt.

Pressing her lips together, she covered Clem's hand with hers. He felt like a Popsicle. "Clem, I can handle this," she assured him and the others.

Her breath came out in little puffs. The ground beneath their feet crunched with a top layer of ice. "You all need to get inside somewhere warm. I can't deal with more than one crisis at a time, and I sure don't want to be having to give you mouth to mouth out here in the cold."

Clem clucked. "Don't get lippy with me, young lady."

She smiled and patted his hand. "I wouldn't dream of it. Now I've got to do my job."

"Seems someone is already taking care of it," Lucy said, pointing.

About ten yards down the beach, a man dressed from head to toe in black and wearing a mask that obscured his face struggled to drag something toward the water's edge.

Audrey narrowed her gaze. Her pulse raced. Amid a tangle of seaweed and debris, she could make out the dark outline of a large body. She shivered with dread. That certainly wasn't a fish, whale or shark. Definitely human. And from the size, she judged the body to be male.

And someone was intent on returning the man to the ocean.

Heart thrumming and adrenaline flooding her body, she took off at a fast clip, but the thirty-two pounds of gear she carried on her person, plus her bulky boots, made maneuvering in the sand difficult. Careful to keep from tripping over clumps of kelp and driftwood that had settled on the beach from the wind and ocean tide, she narrowed the gap.

"Hey!" she shouted. "Stop where you are! Sheriff's department."

The suspect froze, then dropped the prone man's feet in the surf. The perpetrator whipped toward her with a large-caliber gun aimed in her direction.

Her breath caught. She faced her worst fear as an officer.

He fired. And missed.

The sound of the gun blast echoed through the morning air, scattering a flock of seagulls from the water's edge. Fragments of sand pelted her uniform.

Stunned, Audrey dropped to her belly, knocking the wind momentarily out of her. Sand clung to her, getting in her mouth, her nose, as she drew in a breath. She fought through the panic and called on her training. She drew her sidearm. "Halt!"

He ignored her and ran across the sand, heading for the berm separating the road from the beach. She shot at him, the sound exploding in her brain and muffling the world.

He hunkered inward, protecting his head, but kept running. With her ears ringing, she jumped to her feet, torn between giving chase and checking on the man in the sand and making sure Clem and the others weren't hit by the assault.

But the man with the gun posed a threat she needed to neutralize. Now, before he hurt anyone else.

She sprinted after him, kicking up sand with each step while radioing for help. "Shots fired! Officer needs backup."

"Sheriff's on his way!" came Ophelia's barely audible reply through the fuzzy haze inside Audrey's ears.

"Suspect heading toward Prescott Road," Audrey relayed to the dispatcher, praying Ophelia could hear her, since she couldn't be sure how loud or soft she was yelling because her hearing was muffled from the gunfire.

The deep drifts of sand hindered her progress but also the perpetrator's.

Audrey gained on him while trying to aim her weapon. "Stop or I'll shoot!"

Before she could pull the trigger, the suspect reached the berm and disappeared over the top. Tall sea grass obscured him from view. Deep grooves in the sand from his boots were the only sign he'd even been there.

Breathing heavily, Audrey reached the berm and crawled up the sandy embankment in a crouch. She crested the top in time to see a black Suburban peel away from the edge of the road and speed down the street. Before she could get off a shot, the vehicle careened around the corner and disappeared from view.

Frustrated, Audrey pounded the hard-packed sand with a fist. She thumbed her mic while sliding down the sandy berm. "I lost the suspect on Prescott. Black Suburban with missing plates and tinted windows."

She didn't wait to hear Ophelia's answer as she scrambled to the sandy shore and hurried back toward the seawall. "Clem! Mary!"

The four popped up from behind the concrete barrier. "Here!"

Relief nearly made Audrey's knees buckle. "Anyone hit?"

"No, Audrey," Pat yelled back. "You?"

"You okay, Deputy Martin?" Lucy called out.

"I'm good." She did an about-face and ran back to the man lying motionless on the shore. The water lapped at his feet. If she'd arrived any later, the man would be fish bait once again. How had the masked man known where he'd washed ashore?

Keeping her gaze alert, in case the assailant returned, she knelt down next to the supine body, noting with a frown that he was dressed in what could only be categorized as tactical attire, minus the hardware.

Definitely not a fisherman.

And definitely not from around here.

She pressed her fingers against the side of the man's neck, fully expecting to find no pulse, as no one could survive for long in the frigid Atlantic Ocean, not to mention being exposed to the elements onshore. The skin on his neck was like ice, but beneath her cold fingers a pulse beat. Slow, but there!

With a renewed spike of adrenaline, she grabbed the mic on her shoulder. "Send the ambulance to the beach. We have a live one here. Hurry, though!"

"Copy that." Ophelia's surprise matched Audrey's.

Audrey slipped her arms under the man's torso and dragged him to the dry sand. Then she unzipped her jacket, thankful she'd worn her thick, cable-knit sweater over her thermals today, and shrugged out of the outerwear. She laid it over the man on the beach.

Turning to the group of town elders still gawking like she were the main act at the circus, she called out, "Clem, is that your truck parked out there?"

"Sure is," he yelled back.

"Do you have any blankets or jackets? I need them!"

Clem and Pat hustled away, leaving the two older ladies huddled together, staring in her direction. Audrey turned her attention back to the man lying on the sand. Dark hair hung in chunks covering his face. Dried blood matted some of the hair near his temple. He had on black jackboots, similar to the ones she wore, black cargo pants, a black turtleneck and gloves.

She made a quick check for identification. None. She placed a hand on his shoulder. "Lord, I don't know why this man has washed ashore here or what purpose You have, but I pray that he lives. Have mercy and grace on this man. And let us find the masked man without any lives lost. Amen."

The man stirred and moaned as he thrashed on the sand, giving Audrey her first real glimpse of his face as his hair dropped away. Dark lashes splayed over high cheekbones. A well-formed mouth with lips nearly blue from the cold. He had handsome features. Curiosity bubbled inside her. Who was he and what was his story? Why was someone trying to kill him?

"Sir." Audrey gave his shoulder a gentle shake.

A word slipped out of his mouth.

"What?" Audrey bent closer, turning her ear toward his mouth.

"Betrayed..." He stilled and slipped back into unconsciousness.

A sense of urgency trembled through her. What did he mean? Had he betrayed someone? Or had someone betrayed him?

She still didn't hear the siren. Where was the ambulance? It wasn't like the medical center where Sean James kept the bus parked was that far away. Calico Bay was barely the length of a football field. Keeping her gun ready, she stayed alert for any signs of the masked man returning.

Clem and Pat picked their way to her side, their arms loaded with a plethora of blankets and jackets. She quickly packed them around her charge. Whatever this man's story, whether good or bad, she had a sworn duty to serve and protect the community of Calico Bay, and for now that included this man.

The shrill siren filled the air. Good. About time. Within minutes Sean, his intern and the sheriff were hustling across the beach with a stretcher. Sean ambled toward her on an unsteady gait. He carried his medical bag in one gloved hand. A yellow beanie was pulled low over his auburn hair and covered his ears.

His intense brown gaze swept the area as if looking for insurgents. He'd been a medic in the military before losing a leg at the knee when an IUD exploded. The town had been heartbroken at his loss but thankful their star high school quarterback had returned to Calico Bay alive.

Though Sean had slipped into a depression when he'd first come home, the town's people wouldn't let that continue and had pooled their resources to buy the ambulance and make him the town's official EMT.

Audrey moved out of the way to allow Sean and his intern, a kid named Wes, to work on the unconscious man.

"I've got all deputies out looking for the SUV. What do we have here?" Sheriff David Crump asked. He was a big, brawny man with a shock of white hair that had once been as dark as night and a ready grin that had captured her great-aunt's heart back when they were in high school. Now if only Audrey could capture his respect as easily.

She related what she knew.

Sean and Wes rolled the man onto the stretcher. She reached for the edge of the litter along with the sheriff and helped Sean and Wes carry the man to the waiting ambulance. The older folks, still congregating near Clem's truck, watched with avid expressions.

Once the bay doors were closed, the ambulance drove away. The sheriff climbed into his car and took off with his lights flashing. This was going to be big news in town. Audrey moved toward her vehicle, intent on following the ambulance to the medical center. For some reason she felt an urge to stick close to the unconscious man. Probably because he was helpless and at their mercy.

There was something about him that made her think he wasn't going to like being in that state long once he came to. Maybe it was the strength in his chin or the boldness of his cheeks or the width of his shoulders. Or possibly woman's intuition mingled with her cop sense.

"Do you know who he is?" Mary asked, trying to waylay her.

"No, ma'am," Audrey replied and popped open the driver's side door. "You all go home now before you catch a chill. We still have an armed man loose in the township. Be careful and call the station if you see anyone or anything suspicious."

Without waiting for their reactions, she drove through the center of town toward the medical center that served as the town's hospital without turning on her lights. Up ahead the ambulance stopped for a red light at one of only two traffic lights in the town. She stacked up behind the sheriff's car.

When the light turned green, Sean stepped on the gas. The ambulance was in the middle of the intersection when the same dark SUV with a huge brush guard on the front end ran the red light and plowed into the back of the ambulance.

Audrey's mind scrambled to make sense of what she was seeing even as she rammed the gearshift into Park, unbuckled her seat belt and jumped out of her car while once again palming her sidearm. Twice in one day was a new record.

The SUV's tires screeched as it backed up, spun in a half circle and sped off in the direction it had come from. The sheriff's car jolted forward, jumped the curb and took off after the hit-and-run vehicle. Audrey radioed for more backup, then raced to the front of the ambulance. Smoke billowed from the engine block. "Sean! Wes!"

The world tipped and jostled. Pain exploded everywhere. He tried to force his eyelids open, but nothing cooperated. His arms were strapped down. So were his legs.

Where was he? Why was he trapped in some sort of roller coaster? His head pounded. He tried to recall what had led him to this place in time, but a dark void sucked him in. The last thing he heard before the blackness took him back was a woman's panicked voice. He wished he could help her, but he couldn't even help himself.

* * *

Audrey reached the ambulance driver's door just as Sean swung it open. She helped him to the curb. A gash on his forehead bled. Then she ran back for Wes. Thankfully the passenger side door opened easily. The kid was slumped sideways, the white air bag in his lap.

"Let me get the door," a male voice said from behind her.

She nodded gratefully at a local man who'd been passing by on the sidewalk. Once the passenger door was open, Audrey and the Good Samaritan, Jordon, got Wes out. He came with a groan, too, as they sat him beside Sean.

"Jordon, help me with the guy in back," Audrey instructed. The brunt of the impact had been aimed at the back bay. The double doors were crumpled. She let out a growl of frustration and ran to her car's trunk, where she kept a set of Jaws of Life. She'd never needed the equipment before and had hoped never to use it, but she hefted them into her hands, feeling their unfamiliar weight.

The sound of the Calico Bay fire engine rent the air. Momentary relief renewed her energy. Help was on the way. But she had to get inside the bay and make sure the man she'd rescued from the beach hadn't died in the crash, which was no doubt the guy in the SUV's intent.

Before she and Jordon could get into the back bay, the fire truck pulled up. Three men and two women hustled over. Audrey let two of the biggest fire crew members take over with the door.

As soon as the doors on the bay allowed access, she climbed inside. The stretcher had tipped but was wedged between the two benches, providing some protection for the man strapped to the gurney. Thankfully the impact of the SUV crashing into the ambulance didn't seem to have caused the patient any more damage. She checked his pulse and let out a relieved breath.

But someone was determined to kill this man.

And it was her job to keep him alive.

TWO

Audrey finished her after-action report on the shooting and put it on the sheriff's desk—he liked things old-school—but she also sent him an electronic version. Her heart still hammered too fast from this morning's activities. Focusing on the paperwork helped to calm her nerves. But now a bout of anxiety kicked back in. Danger had come to her small part of the world. And she didn't like it one bit.

She stopped by Deputy Harrison's desk. His light brown hair was shorn short, which emphasized the hard lines of his jaw. "Hey, Mike, any idea where the sheriff is?"

"Home, I'd imagine," the thirtysomething deputy replied without glancing up.

She corralled her irritation. He was one of those who weren't comfortable having a female on duty. Earning his respect would be nearly as difficult as that of her great-uncle. Infusing goodwill into her voice—it was Christmastime, after all—she said, "If you see him, would you mind letting him know I'm heading to the medical center to check on our John Doe?"

Mike lifted his gray eyes to her. "Why? The guy's still unconscious. And Gregson's there."

She couldn't explain her driving need to go to the medical center or the need to make sure the man from the beach was safe. So she settled for something the other deputy would understand. "It's my case."

She hurried from the sheriff's station, acknowledging to herself she easily could have called her mom, the primary doctor who was tending to the man they'd rescued on the beach, for an update. But she wanted to see for herself.

Night had fallen several hours ago, and now the world was bathed in the soft glow from the moon and the streetlamps decorated with twinkling lights. A large Christmas tree in the middle of the town park rose high in the air and shimmered with a thousand tiny lights and a brightly lit star.

Normally she enjoyed seeing the tree and the town in the throes of the holiday season, but tonight edginess had her hands gripping the steering wheel in nervous anticipation as she drove.

The news media had picked up the story, reporting an unconscious John Doe found on the beach. The sheriff hadn't released the man's photo. Yet. If the man didn't regain consciousness soon, they'd have to reach out to the public in hopes of identifying the stranger.

No doubt reporters from the bigger towns would descend on Calico Bay and the medical center, making the sheriff's department's job harder. With more strangers in town, finding the masked man would be more difficult. She'd already made calls to all the gas stations, restaurants and grocery stores, asking everyone to keep an eye out for an outsider. In winter, visitors were an oddity in the close-knit community.

Audrey's gaze searched the streets for any sign of trouble, namely in the form of a masked man in black with a large gun. It bugged her no end that the bandit in the SUV had disappeared. The sheriff had chased the offending vehicle for several miles before the creep threw out a handful of spikes that had punctured the sheriff's tires, allowing the suspect to escape. That wasn't an amateur move. Given how the victim and the assailant were dressed, Audrey had a suspicion there was some paramilitary-type thing going on here. Not a comforting thought.

She parked at the side entrance next to her mom's sedan and went inside the brick building, pausing at the nurses' station to ask for her mom.

"Dr. Martin is with a patient at the moment," Katie, the nurse on duty, informed her. Katie shoved her red hair off her shoulder and leaned close. "So was there really a shootout this morning on the beach?"

Resting her hands on the utility belt at her waist, Audrey towered over the other woman. "Yes. No one was hit, thankfully. Where's the man who was brought in this morning?"

"Second floor. Deputy Gregson's on duty."

"Thanks." Audrey bypassed the elevator and took the stairs, preferring to move at her own rapid pace rather than waiting. When she emerged from the stairwell, she halted. Deputy Gregson wasn't at his post.

A bad feeling tightened the muscles of her neck. He should've been sitting outside one of the rooms, but the chair at the other end of the hall was empty. A magazine lay on the floor nearby. She unlatched the strap on her holster and gripped the butt of the Glock as she moved with caution toward the last room.

She passed the nurses' desk. The older woman manning the station glanced up from the report she was studying. "Evening, Deputy."

"Where's Deputy Gregson?"

The nurse popped up from her chair and frowned. "Well, he was sitting right over there last I checked, but

I've been busy so I haven't paid much attention." She sat back down with a shrug. "Maybe he's using the restroom."

"Maybe." Though the itch at the back of Audrey's neck was saying no. Something was wrong. She paused outside John Doe's door, withdrew her weapon, took a calming breath and then pushed the door open.

Lying in the hospital bed, the man blinked at the dark figure towering over him.

The stranger grabbed a pillow, his intent clear as he held the white fluff in both hands and brought it toward the man's face, clearly meaning to smother him. Why would he choose that method of elimination? The answer came with lightning speed. Suffocating him was soundless, providing the goon more opportunity to get away cleanly.

Fear, stark and vivid, flooded his system, short-circuiting his brain in a shower of pain. The patient in the bed lifted his arms to ward off the attack, but his limbs felt heavy. His body responded sluggishly, as if he were fighting to move through mud.

There was no way he could defend himself.

He was about to die. He didn't know why.

His mind reeled. The world receded. His limbs flopped back to the bed at his sides, and darkness claimed him once again.

Several things registered at once for Audrey as she stepped into John Doe's room. Deputy Gregson's prone body just inside the doorway. Blood from a gash on his head.

The same tall, muscular man dressed in dark clothing, with sand still clinging to his boots, stood holding a pillow in his hands, about to suffocate the unconscious man lying in the bed, hooked to a heart monitor and an IV.

"Stop, police!" she shouted.

The intruder spun to face her. The fury in his dark brown eyes, the only thing visible between his black beanie and the black neoprene half mask, was unmistakable when his gaze locked with hers. "You! Not again!" His voice was deep, gruff, muffled by the mask. "Stop interfering."

"Drop the pillow. Put your hands in the air," she commanded, bracing her feet apart in case she had to fire.

He threw the pillow, hitting her in the face and blocking her view for a split second, just enough for the man to use his shoulder to slam into her like a battering ram and knock her off her feet.

"Hey!" She landed on her backside with a jarring thud, her weapon hitting the tile floor and skidding away. The man jumped over her. She grabbed his ankle and hung on, tripping him. He went down, landing on his knees and hands with a grunt. He kicked her with his free foot, his heel smashing into her shoulder.

She ignored the blast of pain and scrambled for a better hold, but he twisted and jerked out of her grasp to race out of the room. She jumped to her feet, grabbed her gun from the floor and dashed after him. He disappeared down the stairwell.

"Call nine-one-one," Audrey shouted to the startled nurse as she raced passed the desk. "Check on Gregson and the patient."

Using caution, Audrey opened the stairwell door and peered inside. She heard the man's pounding footfalls going downstairs. She chased after him, leaping down the last few steps and careening out of the stairwell onto the first floor. Up ahead, the man slammed into an orderly, knocking him sideways, then the assailant hit the exit. Audrey ran outside but lost sight of him.

Not far away an engine turned over, and then tires screeched on the pavement.

Heart pumping with adrenaline, she rushed back inside and up to the second floor. She checked on Gregson, who now was sitting up. A nurse tended to the wound on his head.

"What happened?" Audrey asked the dazed officer.

"I was reading a magazine when someone came out of the room across the hall and attacked me," Gregson replied. "It was a blur. The guy had on a mask, and he hit me in the head with something hard. I didn't see what it was."

With her hand on her gun, Audrey stepped out of the room and pushed open the door to the unoccupied room across the hall. The window was open. She stuck her head out.

Footprints in the dusting of snow on the ledge gave Audrey a pretty good idea of how the perpetrator had gained access—he'd climbed the fire escape and shuffled along the ledge to the window. The lock had been broken. She slammed the window closed and made a mental note to have someone fix the latch as soon as possible.

Audrey returned to John Doe's room and addressed the nurse helping Gregson. "Is he going to be okay?"

"Yes," the woman said. "He'll need a couple of sutures. Dr. Martin will want to examine him to be sure he doesn't have a mild concussion."

"Okay, see that he's taken care of," Audrey said. She put her hand on Gregson's shoulder. "I'll take over the watch tonight. The sheriff should be here any moment. He'll want a full account."

Gregson nodded and looked a bit green around the edges as the nurse helped him to stand and led him out of the room.

Once alone with the unconscious man in the bed, Audrey checked the window, making sure the lock was intact and secure. She took several deep, calming breaths and let the adrenaline ebb away. She'd had more excitement in the past twenty-four hours than since graduating from the academy. She positioned the chair so she had a clear view of the door and the window in case the masked attacker decided to return.

"You're beautiful."

Startled, Audrey whipped around to find herself staring into the dark eyes of John Doe. His lopsided grin sucked the breath from her lungs. She'd never understood the term *roguishly handsome* until this moment. Even groggy and on pain meds, he affected her on an elemental level. Which made her extremely uneasy. What would he be like fully conscious?

Heart pounding, she stepped closer to the bed. "Who are you? What's your name?"

His eyelids fluttered, and he said something unintelligible.

She reached for the button to call the nurse when his fingers closed over her wrist, pressing against her skin where the sleeve of her uniform rode up. His touch was firm but gentle. Strong hands, and calloused, she noted in a bemused way that made her twitchy. She tugged on her arm, hoping he'd get a clue and release his hold. He didn't.

"You look like a Christmas ornament." His words were slurred. "Shiny. Pretty."

His hand dropped away as if he could no longer hold on. His head lolled to the side, and his eyes closed.

"Hey," Audrey said, giving him a slight shake. "Mister, I need you to wake up."

But he'd gone out again.

Okay, that was weird. He'd likened her to a Christmas ornament. Shiny—that was a new one. If she hadn't known he'd been conked on the head and was on mild painkillers, she'd have thought he was on some sort of hallucinogenic. Maybe he was on something stronger than the medical grade medicine. She'd have to ask her mother.

She sat but was too antsy to stay still. She paced at the foot of the bed, every few seconds checking to see if the man had regained consciousness again.

The door opened suddenly, sending her pulse skyrocketing and her hand reaching for her sidearm.

"Whoa, there," her great-uncle's deep voice intoned as he stepped into the room. "Just me."

She relaxed her stance. "Did you see Gregson?"

"Yep. He'll be fine." David moved to the end of the bed and set a fingerprint kit on the chair. "You've saved this man's life thrice now."

Her mouth twitched at her uncle's words. He'd once been a scholar of Old English before giving up academia and carving out a path in law enforcement. "I have a feeling the masked villain isn't going to give up."

He tipped his chin toward the man lying on the bed. "Has he come to?"

"Briefly."

"Did he say anything?"

She hesitated, unwilling to reveal the words that were still echoing inside her head. "Nothing useful. Gibberish. Do you know if a tox screen was done?"

David arched an eyebrow. "You know your mother. Of course that was one of the first things she did."

"Right." Her mother couldn't abide drugs. She'd lost her younger brother to the poison years ago. "And?"

"Clean blood. No track marks."

"Good." For some reason knowing John Doe wasn't a junkie pleased her. But just what and who he was remained a mystery, as did why someone was so ardently trying to kill him. What did John know? "The man who shot at me wasn't some garden-variety bad guy. Whatever John Doe is, he's into something bad."

"Yeah, I have that feeling, too. The road tacks the perp used to stop my car when I chased after him can be bought online easy enough. But there was skill involved."

In the melee of the crash and aftermath, she'd forgotten what John Doe had said on the beach. "He'd muttered a word when I first reached him—*betrayed.*"

"That's interesting. And concerning. The masked man may have been his attacker from the get-go and is very determined to finish the job. I don't like it. I want you to go home," the sheriff said. "I'll stick around until Harrison and Paulson can get here."

She straightened. Did he think she wasn't doing a good job? "I'll stay."

"You've been on duty since five a.m."

"I'm not tired."

He sighed. "Let's get his prints and a photo. Then I'm ordering you to go home. In the morning you can search the criminal and missing-persons databases. Hopefully you'll come up with a name and a reason why someone wants him dead."

Audrey arrived at the station at 6 a.m. and uploaded the fingerprints she'd taken from their mysterious John Doe and his photo off her phone into the FBI's national criminal information center as well as the violent criminal apprehension program for missing persons.

Nothing turned up.

The man could be a Canadian, since the border between the two countries was only a few miles across the ocean. She sent his prints and his photo to the criminal investigation division of the Royal Canadian Mounted Police,

Canada's federal policing agency. She provided her cell phone number so they could contact her directly.

Then she headed back to the medical center to relieve the sheriff. She met Deputy Paulson outside John Doe's room. "How did it go?"

"All quiet," he replied. "Sheriff's inside."

She entered, half hoping John Doe had awakened. He still slept. His face looked relaxed. His dark hair fell over his forehead, covering one eye. Beside him sat the sheriff with his arms folded over his massive chest, his chin tipped down and his eyes closed. Audrey hesitated, debating stepping back out.

"You're here early," the sheriff said softly, lifting his head.

She straightened and came fully into the room. "No hits on NCIC or ViCAP. I sent his info to the RCMP."

"Good thinking." He stood and stretched. "I'm going to grab some coffee. You want some?"

"No, thank you," she replied. His praise eased the worry from the night before that she wasn't doing a good job. Her spine straightened as she moved aside to let him pass.

She went to the window. Frost laced the edges of the glass. She stared at the tree line flanking the west side of the building. The green pine trees were sprinkled with a soft layer of new snow that had fallen during the night. Today, the sun peeked out from behind gray clouds. With 80 percent of the state of Maine forested, there were many hiding places for the masked man to lose himself in. Was he out in the woods now, waiting for another opportunity to strike?

A noise behind her sent a jolt of adrenaline straight to her heart. She spun to find John Doe springing from the bed and landing on the balls of his feet to face her. He ripped out his IV line. It fell to the floor, and the heart monitor sounded an alarm.

Audrey quickly shut off the shrill noise.

The hospital gown they'd put on him stretched across his wide shoulders as his hands went up in a defensive position. Words flowed from his mouth, but she had no idea what he was saying.

She held her hands palms up. Adrenaline flooded her veins. She didn't want to have to take the guy down, but if he didn't calm himself, she'd do it. "Hey, take it easy. You're in the hospital."

More words in a language she didn't understand came at her.

"I don't know what you're saying," she said. "Please speak English."

His panicked dark eyes swept over her and the room. Looking for an escape?

The door behind him opened. A young nurse rushed in, followed by the sheriff, carrying his coffee in one hand. John Doe whirled to confront a new threat.

"Don't!" Audrey shouted, afraid either man would attack the other. "He's okay. It's okay. Everyone's okay."

The sheriff held up his free hand. "Whoa, there, son. No one is here to hurt you. My name is Sheriff Crump. You're safe now." To the nurse, the sheriff said, "We've got this."

She clearly wasn't reassured, as her scared gaze zinged from the sheriff to the patient and back again. "He shouldn't be up. He's bleeding where his IV line was. I should check on his wounds."

Audrey glanced at the smear of blood on the unknown man's arm. The amount wasn't life threatening, just messy.

"You can come back in a bit," David said in a tone that left no room for argument. "I need to question the man."

With a frown, the nurse retreated, leaving them alone

with the mysterious man. John Doe let out a string of words that made no sense to Audrey. Worry churned in her gut. What was going on? Obviously he was a foreigner, but from where? She couldn't place the language.

The sheriff cocked his head, his gaze going to Audrey. She shrugged, at a loss for how to communicate with the patient. The sharp sense of helplessness was too familiar. She hated the feeling. She'd felt this way the night her father hadn't returned from the sea. Only then it had been more intense. Now it was enough to make her jittery.

"I can understand a few words," the sheriff said. "I think he's speaking in Cree. One of the professors I worked with at the university taught a class in Native American studies and had a segment on languages. Cree has a very distinct dialect." He turned his attention back to John Doe. "Does that sound right?"

Confusion played over the man's face. He took a shuddering breath and then spoke in English. "I don't know. I can hear the words in my head, but they mean nothing to me. Where am I?"

"You're in Calico Bay," Audrey supplied. "Were you on a boat?"

John Doe backed up so he could see both Audrey and the sheriff. "I don't know. I don't remember. Calico Bay?"

"Downeast Maine," the sheriff supplied. "The northern tip of the state."

The man kept his gaze on Audrey. "I've seen you before. Where?"

"You woke up for a moment on the beach and again last night while I was here."

John ran a hand through his dark hair. He stilled when his fingers touched the bandage near his left temple. "What happened?"

"We were hoping you could tell us," the sheriff said.

"There've been three attempts on your life since you washed ashore on our beach. Why is someone trying to kill you?"

The man frowned and paced a few steps. "I don't know."

Audrey fought the urge to tell him it would be all right. She didn't know if it would, and she wasn't sure he'd appreciate the platitude.

He staggered to the bed and sat, dropping his head into his hands. "I can't remember anything. Every time I try to recall, my head feels like it's going to explode."

Her heart ached to see his distress. The need to comfort prodded her to take a step closer. The sheriff arched a disapproving eyebrow at her. She halted. Her great-uncle had warned her often enough not to become emotionally involved in cases. She needed a clear, objective head. And if she wanted to be sheriff one day, she had to remain detached and professional at all times.

The patient rolled his shoulders then lifted his gaze to Audrey. "Only your face seems familiar. Nothing else."

The defenselessness on his handsome face tugged at her. She swallowed. Her heart beat erratically. No way was she going to repeat his delirious proclamation that she reminded him of a Christmas ornament. "On the beach you muttered the word *betrayed*. Ring any bells?"

His mouth gaped and he shook his head.

She tapped her fingers against her utility belt. "You can't remember your name?"

He stared at her, the panic returning to his eyes. "No. I can't remember my name. Or who I am. Or where I'm from. I don't know what I meant by *betrayed*." He let out a shuddering breath. "Or why someone wants me dead."

THREE

He couldn't remember his name.

Sitting on the hospital bed under the scrutiny of the deputy and the sheriff made him feel vulnerable. An antsy sort of energy buzzed through him. He might not know his name, but he knew in his gut he didn't do vulnerable.

His body ached everywhere. His head pounded like a jackhammer going to town inside his skull. His mouth felt like cotton. An encompassing terror gripped him. A shiver racked his body. Cold. So very cold. How could he not know who he was? Or recall his past?

Why did someone want him dead?

His heart slammed against his ribs. A looming sense of dread and foreboding threatened to pull him back into darkness. He hung on to the edge of the bed and fought the tug. He needed to stay awake. Some innate knowledge told him he needed to keep a clear head if he were to survive. He grabbed the water pitcher on the bedside tray and poured a glass. He drank it down and then another.

"Then we'll call you John."

"What?" He stared at the blonde, blue-eyed deputy. Her hair was pulled back away from her face and secured behind her head in a knot. She wore little makeup. She didn't need any. She was absolutely stunning with her high cheekbones, delicately carved beneath smooth, unblemished skin and full lips. He forced himself to concentrate on what she'd just stated. "Is my name John?"

It didn't ring any bells. And every time he tried to concentrate, to conjure up a memory, his head felt like someone was taking a pickax to his skull, bringing on a blinding pain that was nearly incapacitating. Only keeping his focus on the beautiful woman's face kept him from keeling over.

She smiled and her eyes filled with compassion. "John as in John Doe. I don't know your name. You weren't carrying identification."

That explained why they didn't know his name. "Where did you find me?"

"The tide deposited you on the public beach early yesterday morning," the man who wore the gold sheriff's badge replied. Sheriff Crump, he'd said. He sipped from his coffee and eyed John with a mix of wary suspicion and empathy.

He'd washed up on the beach like driftwood, which accounted for the bone-deep chill he felt even though the room was heated. Had he been on a boat and fallen overboard? Something else the sheriff said finally registered like a punch to the gut. "You said someone tried to kill me *after* you found me?"

"Yes." The woman told him of the attempts made on his life.

Pressure built in his chest, and his head throbbed. He scrubbed a hand over the back of his neck, hoping to ease the tension that was taking root in the muscles. "I'm sorry about the ambulance. And your patrol car. I'd offer to reimburse you for both, but I've no idea if I have the means to do so." The enormity of the situation weighed him down. "This is all so surreal, like I've walked into a bad horror flick. Has the doctor said how long my mind will be blank?"

"I haven't talked to her yet. We should let her know you've regained consciousness." The deputy reached for the call button.

The deputy smelled like sunshine on a spring day. He breathed in deep, letting an image of a grassy meadow form. Was it a memory or just a generic thought made up of a lifetime of images that had no emotional attachment?

As she moved away, he asked, "What's your name?"

"Deputy Martin," she replied in a brisk tone. She was tall and he'd guess shapely beneath the bulk of her uniform. He'd like to see her with her hair down and wearing a dress that showed off her long legs.

Whoa. Where had that thought come from?

Better to keep his mind on staying alive and not on some errant attraction to the woman who had rescued him from certain death. Pushing the attraction aside, he went with gratefulness. "Thank you, Deputy Martin, for saving my life."

He wished he could do something more for her, but he had no idea what. He had no clothes, no identification and no money. He was trapped in this hospital room until he either remembered who he was or someone claimed him.

Or the man who wanted him dead got to him first.

Anger at the unknown man and dread that he might succeed heated his blood but did nothing to chase away the chill that had settled in his core. Was he married? His heart contracted in his chest. Did he have a family worried about him somewhere? He glanced at his left hand. No wedding band. A sign that he was single or just that he didn't wear a ring? His pulse thrummed in his veins. Frustration drilled into his skull. What kind of man was he?

Why couldn't he remember?

The door opened, and an attractive female doctor wearing a white lab coat walked in. John gauged her age around fifty. Her blond hair was pulled back in a low bun, and she viewed him with bright blue eyes. His gaze darted from the doctor to the deputy. The similarities between the two left little doubt they were related. Mother and daughter?

"Good morning," the doctor said as she hustled forward. "I see you ripped out your IV. Are you in pain?"

He was, but he didn't want meds. "I'm fine. I can handle it."

Her mouth twisted. "Right. You gave us all quite a scare, on many levels. I'm Dr. Martin. What is your name?"

John grimaced. "I don't know. I've lost my mind."

Dr. Martin's eyes widened for a fraction of a second. "You sustained a rather dramatic blow to the head as well as some hypothermia. You have a linear skull fracture that will heal with time. I saw no evidence of a brain bleed. You certainly have a concussion, so you'll need to be monitored for the next twenty-four to forty-eight hours. Most likely the severity of the inciting event coupled with the force of the hit to your temple region caused your memory loss. Retrograde amnesia isn't uncommon. What can you remember?"

"Nothing before waking up here." John darted a glance at the deputy. She'd said he'd awakened last night and that was why she seemed familiar. But he had a feeling she was holding back, not telling him everything. Why would she do that?

The doctor listened to his heart and his lungs, then checked his pupils. "You seem to be in good order. I have no doubt your memories will return. Just be aware that they may come in spits and spurts and be disjointed. Like putting together a jigsaw puzzle. Eventually your memories will slide into place, and you'll be back to your old self."

Foreboding prickled his flesh. Whoever he'd been was someone worth killing. What had he been mixed up in? Something illegal? Was he a criminal? "I shouldn't stay here. Whoever broke in last night might return. I don't want to put anyone at risk."

Deputy Martin's gaze zeroed on the sheriff. "The captain's place. I could take him there."

The sheriff shook his head. "No. The safest place for him, and our town, is a jail cell."

"What!" The deputy shook her head. "No way. We can't lock him up without any evidence of wrongdoing. That would be setting us up for a lawsuit."

The sheriff arched an eyebrow. "Not if putting him in a cell is for his own safety. I know the law, Audrey."

Ah, so that was the pretty deputy's name. John liked the sound of it. He rolled the name around his brain and tried to remember if he'd known her before his memories had been wiped clean, but his mind remained empty, like a void in space. At least thinking about Audrey didn't induce any pain in his head.

Audrey's shoulders dropped slightly, and her mouth pressed into a straight line. "You don't think I can handle this situation?"

The distress in her voice had John tensing. He wasn't sure what was at play between these people, but clearly she had a chip on her shoulder. A strange protective urge surfaced. His hand clenched a fistful of sheet. He didn't know why he wanted to defend this woman. He wasn't sure if she deserved to be defended or not. Maybe she couldn't handle his situation. Maybe she could. But the one thing he did know was he didn't want to cause her harm.

"I didn't say that." The sheriff's tone suggested they'd discussed this conversational land mine before. "But you have to admit, this isn't something we deal with often here in our little corner of the world."

Audrey opened her mouth to reply, but the doctor held up a hand. "David, Audrey, take your discussion outside, please. This is upsetting to the patient."

"No, wait," John was quick to say. "The sheriff's right. The best place for me is somewhere I won't pose a threat to innocent bystanders." Or a pretty deputy sheriff.

Audrey's eyebrows pinched together as she turned her baby blues on him. "You won't be comfortable there. You're recovering from a nearly fatal head wound, not to mention nearly drowning and freezing to death in the ocean."

"Better I'm uncomfortable than anyone getting hurt."

Her gaze narrowed. "That's very self-sacrificing."

"Or very self-serving," John countered. "I have no desire to die. If being locked up keeps me alive until my memory returns, then so be it."

"That's settled," the sheriff intoned. "Carol, when you're ready to release Mr. Doe, I'll take him to the sheriff's station."

Carol's gaze darkened with concern. "If you're sure."

"I am," the sheriff confirmed. "It's best for everyone this way."

Audrey made a distinct harrumph noise but didn't comment.

"I'll have the nurse bring our patient's clothing while I process his discharge papers," the doctor told them. "He'll need careful monitoring to make sure his concussion doesn't worsen. If he loses consciousness again or throws up or complains of dizziness, call me right away."

"We will." The sheriff held the door open for the doctor. "I'll be outside," he said to Audrey before he followed the doctor out of the room.

"That went well," Audrey said on a huff. She offered him a stiff smile. "Sorry you had to witness that little drama."

"What was that about?" he asked. "Are you new to the job?" That had to play into the dynamics between the deputy and sheriff.

She lifted her chin. "Sort of. I did a year on patrol in Bangor before returning home to Calico Bay."

"And how long ago did you return?"

"Less than a year."

Okay. She was inexperienced. The sheriff was being cautious on many levels. John could appreciate that. He'd be the same if he had a fairly new recruit under him.

The thought stopped him. Recruit? What did that mean? Was he in law enforcement? Or was the thought just a random scenario that had nothing to do with his life prior to waking up in the hospital?

The throbbing in his head intensified. His stomach cramped.

"Hey, you better lie down," Audrey said, moving quickly to his side. "You're not looking so good."

"Headache," he said as he scooted back to rest his head on the pillow. "I don't remember the last time I had food."

"You don't want the hospital's grub," Audrey warned. She withdrew a protein bar from the side pocket of her pants. "This will tide you over until we can get you some real food."

Grateful for the snack, he took the bar, ripped open the top and consumed it in three bites and washed it down with another glass of water. The bar hit his stomach with a thud, but it stopped the cramping. "Thanks."

"You're welcome," she said. She rested her hands on her utility belt. "What kind of seafood do you like? It's the season for crab and monkfish now. But mussels are available, as are scallops."

His mouth watered at the thought of some good seafood, but no memory surfaced to support the visceral reaction. "Any of that sounds delicious. You're related to the doctor."

A wry smile curved her lips. "Caught that, did you? She's my mom, and the sheriff's my great-uncle."

"Good to know."

She shrugged. "You were bound to find out eventually."

"I'm not judging. You get flack for being related?"

"Some. But mostly there are those in town who don't think a woman should be on duty. The world is slow to change here in Calico Bay."

He could imagine that was hard for her. She struck him as independent and capable with a soft side that she kept close to the vest. "You said you returned here?"

"Born and raised until I went to college and the police academy."

He admired her commitment to her roots. Did he have roots? He searched his brain until the pain made him back off.

A brunette dressed in scrubs entered the room carrying two bags. "Your clothes." She set the bags on the end of the bed. "Hello, Audrey."

"Morning, Sarah. How's Rich?"

Sarah's face softened. "He's good. He'll be four next week."

"Wow. I hadn't realized." A curious sadness entered Audrey's eyes. "I'll stop by to wish him happy birthday."

"He'd like that. Thank you." Sarah turned to John, her green eyes sharpening with attentiveness. "Do you need help dressing?"

"No. I can manage on my own."

Disappointment shot through Sarah's gaze. "Call me if you need anything."

"Thanks." He was glad when she exited. He met the deputy's gaze. She didn't look pleased. "What's Sarah's story?"

"She's a widow, if that's what you're asking," Audrey replied in a tense voice.

"Okay, it wasn't. I'm more interested in why you looked so sad when you were talking about Rich, who I assume is her son."

Surprise flashed in Audrey's eyes. "Oh. Yes, Rich is her little boy. He's such a sweetie." That sadness was back. "Ben, Sarah's husband, worked on a fishing boat. About two years ago there was an accident, and he was killed."

Sympathy twisted in his gut. "That's too bad. I've watched those fishing reality shows, and that life seems brutal."

Audrey's eyebrows hiked up and anticipation blossomed in her gaze, no doubt hoping his memories were returning. "You remember the show?"

He cocked his head, groping his mind for information. "Yes, sort of. I know I've seen it, but I can't recall where or when." And it was so maddening. He wanted to howl with frustration.

"Give it time," she said as the light in her eyes turned slightly to disappointment. "You heard my mom. Bits and pieces."

"Right." He had a feeling patience wasn't a strong suit of his, but he really didn't know. He opened one of the bags and glanced inside. A pile of dark material pooled in the bottom. Then he looked at the pretty deputy and arched an eyebrow.

"I'll wait outside." Audrey's cheeks pinkened as she walked out.

* * *

Audrey hesitated outside John Doe's hospital room door and tried to calm the flutter in her stomach. So many thoughts and feelings were swirling through her at the moment. Empathy for John Doe. She couldn't imagine losing her memories of her father, her childhood, her life. She could only imagine how bleak and desperate the man must be feeling. Not to mention the pain that seemed to hit him every time he tried to remember.

Then there was the embarrassment of having her mother and John witness the acrimony between her and her great-uncle. She usually did a better job of refraining from showing her emotions in public.

She could only attribute her lack of control to the strange and forceful reactions that flared within her the moment John awoke. Beyond empathy, she felt an intense protectiveness, which had manifested in her strong defense of him. A part of her knew it was logical for the sheriff to take the man into custody, but putting him behind bars without any proof of wrongdoing didn't sit well with her sense of justice.

Hopefully John would soon regain his memories and they could figure out the truth behind what, who and why someone was trying to kill him.

Left alone, John withdrew his clothes and boots from the bags and stared at them for a long moment. He didn't remember putting these on. Why was he dressed all in black? For nefarious purposes?

He was thankful the garments were dry as he quickly donned the cargo pants, turtleneck and socks but struggled with the boots. Finally, giving up, he padded to the door and stuck his head out. Audrey and her great-uncle stood near the nurses' station. The brunette noticed him first and hurried toward him. He tried not to grimace as he held up his hand. "Can you ask Deputy Martin to come here?"

Nurse Sarah pursed her lips, clearly miffed by his request for someone other than her. "Sure." She walked back to the desk and spoke to Audrey, who nodded and headed his way.

"You need me?"

He did. For reasons he couldn't explain she grounded him, anchored him to the moment. When he looked at her, thought about her, he only felt peace, comfort. Strange, considering she'd said they'd only just met. Again that niggling feeing she was keeping a secret from him itched, demanding to be scratched. He let it go, confident he'd get her to open up and tell him. Where that confidence came from, he didn't know. "I need help with the boots. Bending over to undo the laces is more than I can take right now."

One honey-blond eyebrow arched. "All right."

She crouched and undid the laces on the right boot and held it out for him to slip his foot into. He watched as her slender and capable hands quickly cinched up the laces and tied the boot snugly.

After the left boot was on, he stood. The world tilted.

He swayed. Audrey wrapped an arm around his waist and drew him close to her side. If he weren't feeling a bit woozy, he'd have leaned in for a kiss.

He frowned at the thought. Okay, he found Audrey attractive and had some strange connection to her that he didn't understand, but he'd better keep his emotions in check. He could be married. And he doubted the deputy would appreciate him taking advantage of the situation.

Was he a man that took advantage? He prayed not. Which led to another question—was he a man that prayed?

He hated not knowing who he was.

Some part of his brain said to let go of the past and become who he wanted to be for the future. But that wasn't really a possibility. Not when there was someone out there willing to hurt other people to end his life.

He knew deep inside, with a certainty he couldn't deny, he had a responsibility to uncover the truth and to protect those around him.

But he dreaded what the cost would be. He hoped and prayed it wouldn't be the life of the deputy at his side.

FOUR

Sitting in the passenger seat of Deputy Martin's car, John stared at the passing scenery, taking in the quaint and rustic town. The overcast sky washed the world in a gray light. Signs of recent snow collected on awnings and sidewalk gutters. Colorfully painted buildings added cheeriness. Had he seen this village before? If so, had he liked it the way he did now?

There were the usual businesses one would find in any town—a bank, a law firm and a real estate office—but the picturesque storefronts didn't boast any recognizable brand names. Instead, there were places like Melinda's Bakery, the Java Bean, Ted's Fill and Eat.

They passed an Irish pub, numerous fish houses and an art gallery with the name Maine Inspired displaying blown-glass art and paintings in the window. His gaze snagged on the exercise studio advertising dance and fitness classes. He wondered if they had a treadmill and free weights. The need to pump some iron sent nervous energy rippling through him.

"This is a nice place," he commented. Despite the threat stalking him, he felt comfortable in this town. Why was that?

"It's quiet at this time of year," Audrey said. "In spring

the tourists start showing up and don't fully vacate until after Oktoberfest. We have tons of festivals throughout the tourist months. Anything to drive up business to sustain us through the lean season. After Christmas most of the shops and restaurants close for vacations. Some people head to a warmer climate. Others hunker down and wait out the weather."

"What do you do?"

"My job." She lifted a shoulder in a careless shrug. "Though the sheriff insists we all take some vacation, so we rotate through, each taking a week off. Sometimes I stick around to catch up on reading or binge watch movies."

That sounded good to him. "And other times?"

"A warm beach with warm water."

Sun and sand. That sounded good to him. "I could go for a hot day in the Caribbean about now."

She slanted him a glance. "You've been?"

He could picture crystal clear waters, beaches that stretched for miles and sea turtles swimming just below the surface. Memories? Or data stored in his brain from flipping through a travel magazine?

Frustration beat a steady rhythm behind his forehead. "Don't know."

There weren't many pedestrians out on the main street running through the holiday-decorated town. He wondered where he'd be spending Christmas if he hadn't nearly been fish bait. "It's peaceful today."

"Yes. Yesterday's events were very dramatic for our town. Most people are staying off the streets."

A rush of guilt swamped him. "I'm sorry about that. Sorry I washed up on your shore and brought danger to your community."

Audrey brought her patrol car to a halt outside a restaurant called Franny O'Flannery's. She looked him in the eye. "I'm not. The alternative would mean you were dead."

Her words poked at him, reminding him how close he had come to death. And thanks to this woman, he was still here. He unbuckled and put his hand on the door handle.

"Nope," Audrey said. "Stay put. Fran will bring our order to us."

"Curbside service?" he remarked, studying her. Normal or had the deputy asked Fran for the courtesy?

"Perks of a small town. Here we go," she said just as a knock on the window jarred his attention away from her face.

An older woman bent down to peer inside the cruiser. Her lined face was a wreath of smiles and her dark blue eyes regarded him with curiosity. He hit the button on the door panel, and the window slid silently down. A rush of cold air hit him in the face, along with the briny smells of the ocean. But he also caught the aroma of fried food, and his hunger returned with a vengeance.

"Morning, Fran." Audrey leaned over him to talk to the woman at the window, bringing with her a whiff of apple shampoo.

His stomach muscles contracted. His hand tightened around the door handle to keep from reaching up to touch her golden hair.

"Good morning, Audrey," Fran returned. "I see you have a guest."

"Indeed I do," Audrey replied. "This is John. John, Fran O'Flannery. She makes the best crab cakes in the whole state."

Fran grinned. "I don't know about that, but they are popular. Welcome to Calico Bay, John. Are you here on business—" the woman slanted an assessing glance at Audrey "—or pleasure?"

For some odd reason, heat infused his cheeks. Clearly Fran wondered if there was something going on between him and the pretty deputy. "I'm not sure." What business would he have had been doing dressed as a commando wannabe?

"How much do I owe you?" Audrey said before straightening.

Fran handed him the large bag of food. The delicious smells made his insides cramp and his mouth salivate.

"I'll put it on your tab. You can swing by later to settle up."

"Much obliged, Fran," Audrey said. "Give Don my regards."

"Will do. Stay safe." Fran walked back into the restaurant.

"That was nice of her to let you pay later," John commented.

"Yeah, well, she knows where I live." Audrey started up the car and continued to the sheriff's station, a square white building with the fire department on one side and a large steepled church on the other. Audrey parked in front and led him inside, through a lobby where a woman sat behind a Plexiglas window. She waved at Audrey and eyed him with wariness.

John didn't blame the woman. None of them knew what he was capable of, including him. Was he a criminal? He certainly had an element of danger dogging him.

They walked down a hallway with walls decorated with photos of the town. Summer scenes depicted smiling children at a fair. There were pictures of fishing boats with proud fishermen mugging for the camera. The gallery of photos filled him with a strange longing. Was there some place where he belonged? Did he have a community where people knew him? Loved him?

At the end of the hall, Audrey opened a door to a large squad room. A dozen desks, separated by short partition walls, formed a mazelike pattern stretching all the way to the back wall, ending at the closed office door with the sheriff's nameplate. Only four people sat at their desks. They stopped what they were doing to stare at him. He studied each face for a moment but felt no sense of recognition.

Audrey stopped at her desk. He knew it was hers by the collage of photos on her partition. Pictures of her mother and a man he assumed was her father. A family photo with a preteen Audrey, her hair plaited in braids, standing in front of a fishing boat named *Audrey*. A younger adult version of Audrey in a cap and gown. College? Then her in full uniform at her academy graduation.

She pulled a vacant chair over. "Here. Have a seat."

He'd expected her to take him straight to a cell. "Thanks."

She laid out their lunch of crab cakes, tater tots and coleslaw on her desk then took her seat. She bowed her head for a moment, her lips moving silently. Something inside his chest loosened. He followed her example and bowed his head. Lifted up a silent plea. *Lord, bless this food to my body. Heal me. Heal my mind. Amen.*

The crab cakes were as delicious as advertised. "I can't imagine having anything taste better than this."

Audrey wiped her mouth with a napkin before replying. "Right. I'm telling you, Fran's is the best. Her recipe has won awards."

"Tell me about you." He picked up a bottle of water that Fran had also supplied.

"Me?" She shook her head. "Not much to tell."

"Are you married? Kids?" He didn't think so, since there were no photos of her with a man or child, but it felt normal to ask, like something he'd do in his life prior to waking up in the hospital.

Her gaze collided with his. "No to both. What about you?"

His mouth twisted in a rueful grimace. "I wish I knew. You'd think if I were married, if I had a family waiting for me that would be something I'd remember."

"Unless you wanted to forget."

He considered her words. His pulse ticked up a notch. "Maybe that's why I can't remember my past. There's something I want to forget."

"Being hit over the head and thrown in the ocean are traumatic events. Your brain may be protecting you."

"I don't want to be protected. I want to remember." He picked up a tater tot. But his appetite fled.

He hated this not knowing. He had a horrible feeling that something bad was happening, or was going to happen, and he needed to stop whatever it was as soon as possible. Considering there was an assassin trying to kill him, his sense of doom was understandable. But there was something else dancing at the periphery of his mind. Yet when he tried to lock on to the thought, a sharp pain was his reward.

Fatigue dragged at him. He could barely keep his eyes open. "Thank you for lunch, Deputy Martin."

"You're welcome." She canted her head. "You look wrung out. The cell has a cot that I've heard is pretty comfortable."

That comment elicited a smile. "Critiques from past residents?"

She returned his smile. "Something like that."

He liked her smile. It made her blue eyes light up. His gaze drifted down her straight nose to her lush, full lips.

He noticed the slight cleft in her chin that gave her face character.

She rose and held out her hand. "Come on, I'll show where you'll be spending the next few hours."

He stared at her smooth skin and long, slender fingers before grasping her hand. Her fingers closed around his, and she tugged him to his feet. She was surprisingly strong, yet her hand felt almost delicate within his clasp. The dichotomy left him unnerved. He braced his feet apart. The room momentarily swerved then righted itself. Expecting her to let go, he loosened his hold, but for a fraction of a second she held on, her gaze fixated on their joined hands. Then she yanked her hand back and rested it on her utility belt. "This way." She turned and walked briskly away.

He rolled the tension from his shoulders and followed her.

The cell wasn't big by any means, but it was roomy enough and thankfully empty. He didn't relish the idea of sharing the space.

Audrey opened the door. "Sorry about this."

"Don't be." He stepped inside. "This is the safest place for me. No one can get hurt with me in here, and I'll be able to rest without worry."

"I guess." But she didn't sound convinced. That was sweet. He liked that she was upset on his behalf. He wondered if anyone else had ever been upset on his behalf and if so, who?

Needing to reassure her, he moved closer and reached out to tuck a stray strand of blond hair behind her ear. "Are you always so accommodating with your guests?"

"No. But these circumstances are a bit out of the ordinary."

His finger skimmed over her jaw before he dropped his

hand. "I appreciate all you're doing for me. You're a very caring person, Deputy Martin."

He liked the way her cheeks took on a rosy color. "Audrey."

A grin tugged at his mouth. "Okay. Audrey. Such a pretty name for a pretty woman."

Her eyes widened a fraction, then something cold flashed in her gaze and she stepped back. "And you're charming. A flirt."

Wary that he'd offended her, he said, "You say that like it's a bad thing."

"It's been my experience that charming men aren't to be trusted."

Had the man who hurt her been a boyfriend? "Don't paint every man with the same brush as whoever hurt you."

She made a wry sound in her throat. "Easy for you to say. I don't know you. I don't know if I should trust you."

"But you want to," he observed, realizing how badly he wanted her to trust him. "Otherwise you wouldn't have shared your lunch with me. You wouldn't feel so bad for locking me up."

She frowned and pressed her lips into a straight line. He much preferred when she smiled.

"It's okay," he told her. "You shouldn't trust me. I wouldn't trust me."

"I want to release your photo to the media. See if someone comes forward to identify you."

"You should. I'm guessing you already ran my prints and face through your databases."

"Yes, with no results."

He wasn't sure if that was reassuring or more alarming. The thumping in his head intensified. His energy waned. He needed to sit before he fell down. But he didn't want her to leave, which was exactly why he said, "I'm sure you have work to do. And I really need to rest."

She nodded. "I do. I'll be checking on you every two hours."

"I look forward to it."

Without a word, she closed the cell door with a deafening click that echoed in his ears long after she walked away.

Night came faster than Audrey would have imagined, despite the fact that December in Maine the sun set around four in the afternoon. She switched on her desk lamp because the dim overhead lights weren't bright enough for her. The station was quiet. Only a few deputies were at their desks. The sheriff had come and gone, promising he'd be back to relieve her of guard duty for John Doe. She was surprised the sheriff didn't squawk at the overtime she was accruing.

She'd spent the day doing paperwork that had stacked up over the past few weeks. Though she had trouble concentrating on vandalism of the local middle school or Mrs. Keel's runaway cat.

Audrey kept replaying John's words.

Such a pretty name for a pretty woman.

She wasn't sure why his compliment had affected her. Maybe because the first time he saw her he'd thought she was beautiful, like a Christmas ornament. She'd chalked his flirting up to his injury. But earlier he'd been lucid. She didn't trust his flattering words. He was one of those types of men who used their good looks and charisma to their advantage. He might not be able remember his name and his past, but he certainly remembered how to use his charm.

She'd have to be careful around him, because for some unfathomable reason she wanted him to find her attractive.

She gave herself a mental shake. When had her ego hit bottom?

She didn't need a man or anyone else to make her feel good about herself. She was capable, smart and knew what she wanted in life. And it wasn't a charming stranger, no matter how attractive, or what yearnings he stirred.

The radio attached to her shirt came on. Ophelia's disembodied voice came through clear. "Sean is here to see you."

Audrey sighed. She pressed the talk button. "Send him back." She liked Sean, but she wasn't interested in dating him, though he'd asked on numerous occasions. It wasn't that the EMT wasn't handsome or kind or that they didn't get along. They did. As friends. There was no spark between them. She thought of him more as a brother. She and his older sister had been friends forever.

A few moments later, Sean leaned against the partition wall next to her desk. Today he wore jeans and a plaid shirt beneath a puffy dark blue jacket. The stubble on his face matched his dark auburn hair. The only sign he'd been in a car crash yesterday was the purple bruise on his forehead. His searching gaze was trained on her face. "How's it going?"

"So far it's been an uneventful night," she replied. "How are you doing?"

"I've a tough noggin, or so your mother tells me," he said.

"And Wes?"

"Good. Scared. He'd never been in an accident before."

"I'm glad you both walked away with only minor injuries. It could have been so much worse."

"True." He made a face. "The ambulance was totaled. Ted said there was no fixing it."

Audrey trusted Ted's judgment. He'd been a friend of

her father's and had been the town mechanic for as long as Audrey had been alive. "It was insured, right?"

Sean nodded. "Yup. Mayor Grantree was adamant about full coverage when the town bought the ambo. We've already ordered a new one, and the insurance company isn't happy to be paying for it."

Audrey almost felt sorry for the insurance adjustor working the case. Mayor Ginger Grantree was someone Audrey wouldn't want to be on the bad side of. The woman was formidable, and when she wanted something, everybody had better stand back because she was relentless. "I'm glad to hear we'll have a replacement soon."

"How's the guy you found on the beach?"

"He's faring well."

The lights above them winked out. Adrenaline flashed through Audrey. She rose and stared out the large window that showed the lights of the town were on. The outage was isolated to the sheriff's station. The generator would kick in any moment now.

"That's weird," Sean said.

A bad feeling prickled the skin at her nape. "Yes. Too weird."

Just as the generator brought up the emergency lights, Harrison stepped out of the men's restroom. Audrey could make out his silhouette.

"What's happening?" Harrison's voice reverberated with unease.

"Don't know," she replied. "Sean, stay with Harrison. Get Ophelia and get to safety."

She hurried toward the back where John Doe was locked in a cell. In the time she'd worked for the sheriff's department, the electricity had never failed without cause. She could only assume the man after John Doe was behind the outage. She reached the cell door. She couldn't make out John in the dark. She reached for the keys attached to her utility belt.

A loud explosion rocked the building.

FIVE

John jerked awake to a cacophony of noise. Emergency sirens bounced off the cell walls. He heard shouted voices. Heart pumping with a jolt of adrenaline, he rolled from the cot, landing soundlessly onto the balls of his feet in a crouch. Every muscle tensed in anticipation. Fight or flight? Not flight. He was trapped in a cell. He scanned the darkness, momentarily disoriented. He'd been lying with his feet facing the cell door. Staying low, with his hand stretched out before him, he moved toward where he thought the door was located.

"John?" Audrey's call rang in his ears.

Relief tempered the adrenaline racing through his veins. "Here."

A beam of light swept over the cell and landed on him.

He wrapped his hands around the cold steel of the bars. Though he couldn't see her behind the glare of the flashlight, the rapid pace of her breathing pinpointed her location. "What happened?"

"Someone killed the lights. The explosion was likely the generator." The flashlight bobbed. The rattle of keys echoed in the cell, then he heard the faint squeak of a hinge as the door opened.

Warm, strong hands grasped his and pulled him toward the back exit. "Come on. We're getting out of here."

He tugged her to a halt. "They'll be expecting us to go out the door. It'd be too easy to pick us off." He wasn't about to let her put herself in the line of fire. She might be a deputy sheriff, but it was his head they wanted, not hers.

"So we wait for them to come blazing in? I don't think so."

He didn't like that option any better. "Are we the only ones in the station?"

"No. We have to get everyone out alive."

"Are there only two exits?"

"The break room window. It drops onto a strip of grass between this building and the community church." She tightened her hold on his hand. They ran back to the squad room, where another deputy held a flashlight illuminating a male civilian and the woman John had seen behind the glass in the lobby.

"I've called the sheriff," the deputy announced to the people next to him. "He's on his way. We're safe here. The fire department has the fire under control in the back parking lot."

The deputy turned suddenly, his hand going for his sidearm as John and Audrey approached.

Audrey dropped John's hand. "Whoa, Harrison. It's me."

"Audrey, what's happening?" the woman said, her voice shaky with panic.

"I don't have answers yet, Ophelia," Audrey told her. "But we need to get out of here. But not through the doors. We'll go out the break room window and hide inside the church."

"You think the explosion was deliberate?" the younger guy asked.

"Unfortunately, Sean, I do," she replied. "It's the same person or persons who crashed into the ambulance."

John didn't like the way Sean moved to Audrey's side in a clearly possessive way. She'd said she wasn't married and had no kids but hadn't mentioned if she was involved with someone. Though why John was upset didn't make sense. He could very well be married or engaged or involved with someone he couldn't remember. Until he knew his past, he couldn't contemplate a present or future that included anyone else.

Needing to act and not let his mind play games with him, he said, "We should hustle before the perps decide to storm in."

"This way." Audrey grabbed the sleeve of his shirt and tugged him closer. "Stay behind me."

Though he appreciated her protectiveness, it felt wrong. He should be the one going first, blazing a trail for her to follow. His empty hand flexed with the need to feel the weight of steel pressed against his palm. He tucked the thought away to examine later as he did as the very determined female deputy directed. Sean, Ophelia and the other deputy fell in line behind them, with the deputy taking up the rear position.

Inside the break room, Audrey released her hold on his sleeve and went to work on prying out the window screen. He helped her and took it from her hands to set aside.

"I'll go first to make sure it's clear," Audrey said. "John, you follow me. Then the rest of you."

"I'll go first," the other deputy blurted before John could.

"Harrison, I need you to protect our flank. You're a much better shot than I am." Audrey's voice had lowered to a measured beat.

John arched an eyebrow at her placating tone, meant

to both defuse a potential issue and bolster the deputy's confidence at the same time.

Deputy Harrison ate up her words and totally missed the subtle undertone. "You're right. I'll make sure you all get to safety."

Audrey didn't waste any more words but slipped quickly and soundlessly out the window. John had to give her major credit for getting her way without causing a rift. He wondered if it were true that Harrison was a better shot or if she was downplaying herself for the deputy's benefit.

He leaned into the open window. Moonlight from the full winter moon revealed that there indeed was a wide strip of grass separating the sheriff's station from the side of the church. The white-painted wood building gleamed in the moon's glow. He could smell the acrid smoke of the burning generator.

He spotted Audrey right away—her darker form outlined against bushes growing along the church's side yard as she motioned for him to follow her out the window. He climbed over and dropped to the ground. The grass beneath his boots was crusted in ice and crunched beneath his weight.

He turned to help the dispatcher, Ophelia, out of the window. She hopped out of his hands as soon as her feet touched down. When Sean swung one leg over the side of the windowsill, his pant leg rode up, revealing a metal prosthetic above the tennis shoe.

John's heart twisted with empathy. He reached out a hand to help the man. After a moment of hesitation, Sean grasped John's hand and slipped out the window. John steadied the guy then let go.

"Thanks, dude," Sean whispered.

Deputy Harrison came through the window less gracefully. He grunted when he hit the ground. John grabbed him by the arm to keep him from going down on his rear.

"Hurry." Audrey's voice carried on the slight breeze coming off the ocean.

John ushered Ophelia and Sean to her side. She led them to a wood door in the side of the church.

Harrison reached past her to try the handle. "It's locked."

"Give me a second," Audrey shot back. She shuffled through the keys on her key ring. "Pastor Wilson gave me a key."

"Why?" Harrison demanded to know. "I didn't get a key."

Seeing that Harrison wasn't watching their six, John took a position with his back facing the church so he could see both entrances of the side yard. His hands flexed again, and the urge to hold cold metal against his palm was strong. Sean moved to stand beside him. Curiosity about the man burned in John, but now wasn't the time.

A movement to the right caught John's attention. His muscles tensed. The shape of a tall man carrying an automatic weapon was clear for a moment before a shadow swallowed him up.

"Combatant at three o'clock," Sean whispered.

"I see him." John had to deal with this. He couldn't let these people get hurt. "Make sure they all get inside," he said at a level barely considered a whisper.

Keeping to the shadow of the building, John made his way toward the armed man. Moving on instinct and some buried muscle memory, John prepared for hand-to-hand combat.

His first priority would be to disarm then disable. He mentally pictured the tactics for neutralizing his opponent.

As he closed in on the man, John heard the faint, telltale sound of boots on the ground behind him.

He flattened himself against the wall just as Audrey bumped into him. He knew it was her by the fresh apple scent of her hair. He ground his teeth together. She needed to be inside, where she was safe.

A foot away the masked man stopped, as if sensing he wasn't alone.

John held his breath. He didn't know what Audrey planned. He didn't like being out of sync with his partner. They needed to be of one mind for an assault to work. That he considered her as a partner was something he'd deal with later.

He touched Audrey's hand. Using his index finger, he tapped her palm twice, though what he was trying to convey to her lurked beyond his mental reach. Frustration crimped the muscles in his shoulders. They were going to get themselves killed.

Audrey's fingers curled over his and pulled him toward her, obviously wanting him to go with her to the safety of the church. He resisted. This could be their only chance to catch this guy. She elbowed him lightly before she squeezed his hand and then stretched her arm to the left in a semicircle. Then she moved their joined hands to his chest and thumped. He squeezed her hand, not comprehending her message.

She thumped him again and then stretched her arm past him to the right. It dawned on him that she wanted him to go behind the man while she confronted from the front. He didn't like it. He brought her hand to his face and shook his head no.

She released her hold on him and broke away. She was going to take this guy on herself.

Gritting his teeth, he made a wide sweep so that he ended up behind the perp.

A bright spotlight beamed on the man. "Halt, sheriff's department. Drop your weapon."

The man brought his rifle barrel up. John slammed into him from behind, wrapping his arms around his torso and trapping his arms at his side, making it impossible for the man to fire at Audrey, as they went to the ground with John landing on top of the intruder.

John swiftly sprang up enough to dig his knee into the man's back, keeping him glued to the ground while he wrestled the guy's hands behind his back.

Audrey was there in a flash with a set of handcuffs. John slapped them over the man's wrists and secured him in a tight hold. He patted him down by rote, vaguely aware that some part of his brain had given the command.

He found a money clip holding some cash and a blank key card. No other weapons and no identification. A shudder worked over John. He'd washed ashore dressed nearly the same, also without ID. Had John and this man worked together? If so, why was this guy trying to kill him?

He yanked the man to his feet. Audrey grabbed the man's rifle from the ground. The sheriff and several other deputies rounded the corner of the building with their flashlights aimed at them.

"Audrey!" The deep timbre of the sheriff's concerned voice rang out. "You okay?"

"Yes, sir." She stepped close to John. "Good job."

"Thanks." He relinquished custody of the criminal to Audrey. To the sheriff, John said, "There might be more of them."

The sheriff instructed the half dozen officers to spread out and search the area. The door to the church opened. Deputy Harrison came out, followed by Ophelia and Sean.

"All right, everyone," the sheriff said. "Let's take this back inside the station."

"They blew the generator," Harrison said. "The station's dark and the fire department's on the same electrical circuit, so it's dark, too."

"Paulson," the sheriff called.

A deputy hustled over. "Yes, boss."

"Get someone out here to fix the generator and the electricity," Sheriff Crump commanded. Turning to the group huddled around him, he said, "Let's take this inside the church. Harrison, call Pastor Wilson, let him know what's up."

"On it." Harrison moved away to use his cell phone while the sheriff ushered them all inside the church.

Someone flipped a switch and wall sconces lit up, dispelling the inky shadows and revealing a small wood-paneled room with several doors. The sheriff pushed open a set of doors to the left and led their suspect into an office. He pushed him into a chair and took the black beanie from his head, revealing cropped sandy-blond hair.

John moved so that he could face the man. He was a stranger to him. Or at least John assumed, since he felt no recognition at all. The man had wide-set eyes, broad features with a nose that had been broken in the past and a jutting chin. "Who are you? Why are you trying to kill me?"

The man stared through him. "I'm not talking to you," he said in a softly accented voice.

Eastern European. John didn't question how he knew. John stalked to the window, careful to keep the majority of his body out of the line of sight in case the suspect had a cohort who might want to take a potshot at him. He stared out at the parking lot shared by both the church and the sheriff's station. The glowing embers of the burned-out generator and the dozen or so firefighters in turnout gear were visible.

"What do we do now?" Ophelia asked. "Ed will be wondering where I am."

"Deputy Harrison will take you home," Sheriff Crump said. "Sean, you need to go on home, too."

John turned from the window, his gaze on the man in the chair. "Is it safe for them to leave?"

The man shrugged but held his gaze. "They're not the target."

A fist of dread hit John in the solar plexus. "Right. I am."

Sean's gaze bounced to Audrey. "Are you sure you'll be okay?"

"I'm fine, Sean," Audrey assured him. "Tell Jessie hello for me."

John heard the faint thread of annoyance in her tone and again wondered what exactly her relationship with the younger man was.

Sean nodded, but there was no mistaking the frustration on his face as he left with Ophelia and the deputy.

Sheriff Crump sat on the edge of the large desk dominating the office. "It would be helpful if you told us your name since we're all going to be here for a while."

"Sasha," the man said with a shrug. "My name is Sasha."

Audrey stepped closer. "Thank you, Sasha, for telling us your name. Do you know his name?"

Sasha's lip curled. "No."

"Are you hungry?" she asked, fishing around in her cargo pants pockets and producing a protein bar.

Sasha shook his head.

"Thirsty?" She walked to a small refrigerator in the

corner. "Pastor Wilson keeps water here." She pulled out bottles of water. "Sheriff? John?"

"I'm good," replied Sheriff Crump.

Seeing the sharp way Sasha stared at him, John nodded. "Sure. I'll take one." What John really wanted was to shake the man and force him to talk, but he knew torture in any form wouldn't give the desired results, so he followed Audrey's lead to build a rapport with their suspect. "What about you, Sasha? A cold bottle of water?"

Sasha looked away and shook his head.

Audrey walked back with two bottles of water and handed one to John. "You know, Sasha, at the moment all we have you on is assault with intent to do bodily harm by pointing a loaded weapon at an officer. We can't prove you blew up the generator. If you help us by telling us who and why someone wants this man dead—" she pointed to John "—we can help you."

Sasha snorted. "You can't help me. I'm dead. Just like he's dead."

His pronouncement shuddered through John.

"We can protect you," she insisted.

The door to the office opened, and Paulson stuck his head inside. "The electricity's back on."

Sheriff Crump straightened and took Sasha by the arm. "Come on, I've got a jail cell waiting for you."

The sheriff led Sasha out the door.

Audrey met John's gaze. The anxiety in her eyes had him stopping in his tracks.

"He's not the man from the hospital."

John's heart slammed to a halt. "What?"

"The man at the hospital didn't have an accent and was leaner." Her grim tone constricted his lungs. His stomach dropped. There were more bad guys out there determined to kill him.

A shout from outside drew their attention. They ran to the door. The sheriff and Paulson had their guns drawn and their flashlights lighting up the dark as they stood back to back. Sasha lay on the grass.

Immediately John grabbed Audrey, dragging her farther into the shelter of the windowless vestibule. "Kill the lights."

Audrey hurried to the wall panel and flipped the lights off, shrouding the church in darkness.

"Where'd the shot come from?" Crump demanded.

"I don't know," Paulson responded in a high-pitched tone full of panic.

John crouched in the doorway. "Sheriff, you two need to find cover."

The sheriff knelt on one knee and checked Sasha's neck. John already knew the sheriff wouldn't find a pulse. Sasha had been dealt a catastrophic head shot directly to the brain stem. He was dead before he hit the ground. Just as John would have been if he'd stepped outside the church.

SIX

"I have to leave," John said, barely able to discern Audrey's outline in the darkened vestibule. They stood inside the door, careful to stay in the shadows and out of the ambient light coming from the moon outside the church. His gut clenched. Leaving was the only answer. "I can't stay here. I'm putting you and your town in danger."

"I know. I've got to move you to a more secure location." The hard determination in her tone came at him through the shadows.

He frowned in the dark and shook his head. She didn't get his meaning. "Not *with* you. I have to go on my own. I can disappear."

"No." Her voice was adamant. "That's not happening."

Her stubbornness could get her killed. "It will be safer for you."

"Don't make this about me." She stalked forward until she was standing in front of him. He could feel the heat of her annoyance buffeting him. He could imagine her blue eyes sparking and wished he could see her face.

"I'm a professional and I have a job to do," she insisted. "Part of that job is protecting you. I'm not letting you take off alone. You don't have any money or ID. And unless you plan to become a criminal, you're not getting either one."

He hated to admit it, but what she said was true. Frustration banded across his chest. "How do you know I'm not already a criminal? I'm dressed exactly like Sasha."

She let out a little noise of irritation. "Black clothes don't make you a criminal."

He had to make her see his point. "But I could be. You said I'd muttered a word when you found me on the beach." He reached out, and though it was too dark to see her, his aim was true. His hand gripped her shoulders. "Do you remember what I said?"

"Of course. *Betrayed.*"

The word hung between them, sending a shudder down his spine.

"Then doesn't it stand to reason that whomever I betrayed is after me?" He released her to pace into the inky corner. "And if I betrayed someone who has the means and the mind-set to hire guns to kill me, I'd say that there's no doubt a criminal element is at play here and I'm smack-dab in the middle."

"I agree there is a criminal element at work." Her voice took on that soothing, you'll-do-as-I-want tone he'd heard her use on others.

A smile tugged at the corners of his mouth despite himself. She really was something, this beautiful and determined deputy.

"But until you're proven to be a criminal, I have to consider you a witness and a victim." Her words were a punch to the gut.

He let out a scoff. "I'm a victim, all right. A victim of a defective mind."

"Can you hold off on the pity party until we get out of here?"

He barked out a laugh. The woman never gave an inch. He liked that about her.

Audrey drew in a breath. "John, you also have to consider the fact that someone might have betrayed you."

The darkness pressed in on him. Had someone betrayed him? Was that what this was all about? The reason someone wanted him dead? His fingers curled into a tight fist.

Audrey's cell phone lit up as she dialed the sheriff. She covered the screen with her hand to mute the light. The ringing of the sheriff's phone placed him still in the side yard. Audrey put the phone on speaker when the sheriff answered.

"I'm taking John out of here through the tunnels," she informed him. "Then I'm driving him to the captain's."

Where exactly was this captain located? And what tunnels? John kept his curiosity in check. He'd ask later.

There was a moment of silence before the sheriff responded. "That's probably the safest place. I'll send Paulson with you and then I'll relieve him tomorrow."

"Fine. Tell Dan to go home and pack a bag. Ask him if he has anything that might fit John," Audrey said. "John and I will swing by and pick him up in an hour after I've stopped by my place."

"Copy." The sheriff hesitated before adding, "Audrey, be careful."

"Of course." She hung up and grabbed John's arm and slid her hand down until she clasped his hand. "Come on. We're leaving."

He allowed her to pull him from the vestibule to one of the double doors. "Uh, how exactly are we getting out of here?"

"Have you ever heard of the Embargo Act of 1807?" She led him into the sanctuary.

"Couldn't tell you one way or another."

"Right. Okay, fair enough." Moonlight streamed through the high stained glass windows, allowing enough multicolored shards of light for them to weave their way through the pews toward the front of the church. "Construction on this church began in 1805 and was finished in 1810. In the year 1807, President Jefferson imposed an embargo on foreign trade that lasted for two years. Needless to say the whole Down East was hit hard. The small settlement at Calico Bay was in jeopardy of disappearing. Being that people still needed to export and import goods, the craftsmen working on the church devised a plan. They proceeded to build a tunnel under the church that extends all the way to the cliffs."

She knelt in front of the altar and patted the floor. He squatted next to her. "Lose something?"

"I'm looking for the handle. It's inlaid into the wood."

"Handle?"

"Smuggling goods to and from ships anchored off the coast was how people survived. Then the War of 1812 happened, and the tunnels were used by the militia to defend the bay. Aha. Found it."

"How do you even know the tunnels are still there?"

"I grew up in this town, remember? I've explored every inch of the tunnels, the cliffs and the forest on the west side of the town." She planted her feet and grasped the handle to lift a two-by-two hatch carved into the floor. "Grab the edge."

He did as she asked, easily lifting the lid all the way. He peered into darkness below. He thought he heard a rustling sound. Were there snakes in Maine? An image from a movie slammed into his mind. The hero of the action flick fell into a pit of snakes. A shudder of revulsion vibrated outward from John's core. Why could he remember a movie and not something important like his name or his life?

"There's a ladder" she said. "We'll have to go by feel

until we close the hatch. I don't want to use my light until we're safely below ground."

She sat on the ledge and felt around with the toe of her boot until she found the ladder rung. "Got it." She held out her hand. "Sit next to me."

John slipped his palm flat against hers. Warmth shot up his arm from the point of contact. Her fingers entwined with his as he settled on the edge.

"Can you balance the hatch while you go down the ladder?" she asked, her voice oddly breathless.

"I can manage that."

She slipped off the ledge and disappeared into the pit below. After a few moments, she called out, "Okay, start down."

John used the toe of his boot to find the rung of the ladder, then he climbed down, slowly allowing the hatch to close behind him, blocking the moonlight until only darkness remained. His hands tightened on the rung as his foot touched the ground. Audrey flipped on her flashlight, illuminating a long tunnel carved through the earth and bolstered by thick wooden beams.

Damp, earthy scents filled his nose, making him itch. An uneasy shiver worked its way through him. He decided he wasn't fond of enclosed places. "Are you sure this won't collapse on us?"

She laughed. "Yes, I'm sure. This way."

They traveled through the dark, dank tunnel for several yards. A rodent scurried along the ground beside him.

They finally came to a wooden door with large black hinges and a lever latch that let out a loud squeak as Audrey lifted it. Then she pushed the door wide enough for them to slip through.

They were at the base of a cliff just north of the beach where John had washed ashore. He breathed in deep of the salt-tinged air, liking the refreshing way it cleared off the itch to his senses and made his chest expand. Definitely more comfortable in open spaces.

Audrey walked away from the water to a berm separating the beach from the street. John followed, the sand making his gait unbalanced. He paused to turn back to the sea, his gaze on the churning ocean. Moonlight danced on the white-crested waves that undulated with the rough current. The lights of Canada twinkled in the distance like little beacons.

Audrey retraced her steps to his side. "John?"

Could he have washed ashore from the country across the bay? "Have you heard from the Canadian government?"

"Not yet. You have to be patient."

"I wonder if patience is one of my virtues."

She tucked her arm through his and steered him toward the road. "Patience takes discipline. There may be people who are born with an extra dose, but it's been my experience that patience takes effort. We've become too much of an instant-gratification world."

Staying to the shadows, they walked at a steady pace down the quiet residential street to the main street. Audrey led him to a steep staircase behind the mercantile. "My apartment's up here."

He followed her up the staircase, curious to see how this woman lived. "You don't live with your mom?"

"No. She lives in a cottage near the medical center." She unlocked the door and stepped inside.

He entered the studio, taking in the very feminine decor. Bright color spots popped against earth-toned furnishings. She'd carved out very distinct sections in the open studio space.

Just inside the entrance was the kitchen and eating area.

Whitewashed cabinets and stainless steel appliances took up one wall, while a small antique-looking table with folding sides and two wooden lattice-back chairs sat across from the stove and sink.

For the living space, a well-loved sofa with plush throw pillows butted up against the exterior wall, and a glass coffee table sporting a stack of books sat on a round area rug covering hardwood floors.

On the opposite wall above a six-drawer dresser, a television had been mounted on a swinging arm so that she could watch from the sofa or from the full-size bed decked out in shades of purple and pink bedding.

A small vanity table laden with jewelry and makeup paired with a curved-back chair sat next to a door that he assumed led to the bath. The whole effect was impressive. She'd made the most of the tight space.

"This is nice," he commented out loud. "Homey." He couldn't help but wonder what his accommodations were like. Did he live in a studio apartment or a house? Did he share his living space with someone? A wife? A roommate? Or did he live alone? He rubbed at the biting sting at his temple.

"Thank you," Audrey replied. "I like it."

She pulled a duffel bag from beneath the bed then proceeded to throw some clothes from the dresser into it. She grabbed a few items from the bathroom. After zipping up the bag, she lifted the strap and dropped it over her shoulder. "All set."

"Let me take that," he said, reaching for the strap.

She stepped back. "I'm capable of carrying my bag."

He held up his hands. "Whoa. I didn't think you weren't. Just trying to be a gentleman."

Embarrassment charged across her face. "Sorry. I don't mean to be testy. I'm always having to prove myself, and sometimes I forget that I can allow someone else to do things for me."

"You don't have to prove anything to me," he assured her. "I've been impressed with you from the moment I awoke in the hospital."

Her gaze narrowed slightly as if she weren't quite sure she should believe him. He remembered her disdain of charming men. He wanted to smash in the face of the man who'd hurt her.

"We should get moving," she said briskly. "My car's parked on the street."

He nodded and followed her out of the apartment. Her car was a beautiful early-model Mustang GTO in a metallic blue. The charcoal-gray interior looked brand-new. The passenger seat was comfortable. She started the engine, and the beast of a car growled. "Sweet ride."

She pulled away from the curb and headed away from the main drag. "I love this baby. I saved up for years before finally finding the right one. It has a V8 engine and had very low mileage when I bought it."

"Not very stealthy," he commented at the rumbling beneath the floorboards.

"Yeah, well, I hadn't expected I'd need stealth. But it will pretty much outrun any other car on the road."

"You sound sure. What about in the snow?"

"Snow tires." She turned down a residential street.

"Doesn't seem like a practical car."

"I manage in the winter. I keep the trunk weighted." She grinned at him. "I take this baby to the racetrack in Bangor during the summer."

For some reason he wasn't surprised. She struck him as a woman who liked adventure. "That sounds fun."

"It is." She brought the car to a halt in front of a box of a house trimmed in twinkling blue and white lights.

An inflatable snowman stood sentry on the front lawn, and behind the front window curtains was the outline of a Christmas tree.

Deputy Dan Paulson hustled out of the house with a bag slung over his shoulder and carrying a thick jacket, which he thrust into John's hand when John jumped out to push the backrest forward so Paulson could climb into the small backseat. It was a good thing it would only be the three of them, because no way could another person fit back there.

"Sheriff said we're going out to Quoddy Head," Paulson remarked as she gunned the engine and they took off.

"Yep. I know a safe place." She turned onto the highway heading away from the ocean.

"Is this where the captain lives?" John asked.

She chuckled. "Not anymore. But fair warning, it's rustic."

John studied her profile, liking the curves and angles of her face. "How rustic? As in no restrooms? No heat?"

"Not that uncivilized. No internet, no cell service."

No biggie for him. He didn't have a cell phone or a computer.

Paulson nearly sputtered. "But what if we need help? How do we contact the sheriff?"

"Satellite phone," she replied. "Don't worry, Paulson. There's no way anyone will be able to find us out there."

"Yeah, from your mouth to God's ears," the other deputy groused and sat back.

"Amen to that," John said. He sent up a quick prayer that whoever was after him didn't know about this place. Audrey exited the highway onto a two-lane road that stretched out before them with dense woods on either side. Snow covered the forest floor. Occasionally John checked the side-view mirror to make sure there were no other cars traveling in the same direction. The longer they drove, the denser the foliage became.

Suddenly beams of light appeared behind them.

Adrenaline pumped through John's veins. What were the chances that someone else would be out on this road at this time of night? How had they found them? "We've got company."

The lights gained on them. The hairs on the back of his neck jumped to attention. This was no casual driver out for an evening drive.

"Hang on," Audrey warned. She cranked the wheel and sent the car into a spin. She straightened the wheel when they were facing the oncoming car.

"What are you doing?" Paulson shouted. "Are you crazy? This isn't a time to play chicken."

"I'm not," she replied in a tight tone. "Normally we'd be dealing with a couple feet of snow at this time of year, but it's late in coming. We have only a dusting to make things slick."

Facing the oncoming vehicle allowed John to determine the rapidly approaching car was an SUV. A monster of a thing with a large brush guard, looking a bit beat-up.

"It's them," Audrey said. "The men who are trying to kill you."

Grabbing onto the dash, John asked, "What are you doing?"

"I told you this can outrun anything," she said. "That beast of a machine won't be able to turn around quickly enough to follow us. We'll be taking a more scenic route."

The distance between them and the oncoming SUV lessened. John gritted his teeth. He had to trust Audrey. Trust that she knew what she was doing, because he and Paulson were at her mercy.

Blinded by the SUV's headlights, he braced himself for

impact, but at the last second, Audrey swerved, roaring past the SUV. She floored the gas, and the Mustang raced away, the studded tires thumping on the snow-crusted road. She shut off the headlights and the interior dash lights, plunging them into darkness.

"Hold on, because there's a turn up here and I'm going to make it without braking," she said.

From the backseat Paulson groaned. "You're going to kill us."

"Have a little faith, Paulson," Audrey shot back. Her heart pumped a frantic rhythm beneath her breastbone. Her hands gripped the steering wheel. She eased her foot off the gas. The car incrementally slowed. How had they found them? Her mind grappled with possibilities. Something that had been bugging her roared to the center of her mind.

How had the bad guys known where to find John when he'd washed ashore? And then when exactly to hit the ambulance?

She downshifted and cranked the wheel, smoothly taking the turn into a break between two copses of trees, and brought the car to an abrupt halt.

"John, check your clothes and your boots for a tracker."

"Tracker?" His voice held a glint of surprise. "Of course."

John searched his clothes and gritted his teeth through the pain as he finally yanked off his boots, inspecting them. "Found it." He rolled down the window, allowing the frigid air to swirl through the interior of the car while he chucked the tracking device out into the woods. "It was embedded in the heel of my boot."

Gratified and yet mad at herself for not thinking of it sooner, she pressed on the gas and they bounced along on a rough road with only the moonlight as their guide. A layer of snow that had crusted into ice crunched beneath their tires and twinkled in the moonbeams. She kept the car at a moderate speed, compared to how she'd been driving.

"Do you know where you're going?" Paulson asked in a shaky voice.

"Of course. I know every inch of these woods," she said. "Besides, there's no way for them to know where we're heading now."

After ten minutes and no sign of being followed, she flipped on the headlights, illuminating the trees and the snow covering the ground.

The dirt road ended at a T. She slowed and took the turn to the right. They headed down another road, barely wide enough for the car. A pristine layer of white covered the swath of road, which ended at a large circle.

She parked and popped open her door. The crashing of waves on the rocky shore could be heard even though she couldn't see the ocean from where they were. "Okay, boys, we're hiking from here."

"Hiking to where?" Paulson asked from the backseat.

She twisted around to look at him. "The lighthouse."

Paulson scoffed. "I thought you said you knew a safe place out here. I thought you meant a nice warm vacation home."

She held back a smile. "The lighthouse is safe."

Paulson shook his head. "And if they decide to look for us at the lighthouse, then what?"

"We'll see them long before they reach us," she told him. "And if we need it, there's a dory we can use."

"A dory?" John opened his door.

"A small flat-bottomed boat," she answered. "There's one docked at the lighthouse."

"Great," Paulson groused. "We can be ducks in a boat. And if the bad guys don't do us in, the ocean will."

"Relax, Dan. The dory has a motor." She climbed out of the car and shut the door. She flipped up the collar of her uniform jacket and regretted they couldn't have driven right up to the lighthouse.

John climbed out, slipped on the borrowed jacket and then hustled to the back of the car to pick up Audrey's bag from the back hatch. "You lead the way," he told her.

She hesitated, fighting her need to be independent. "Thank you." She flipped on her flashlight. "We're going to be forging our own trail until we meet up with the official one."

They hiked for an hour through dense trees and bushes before they came to an actual trail carved through the forest. Then they followed that trail until they reached an area with darkened outbuildings surrounding the lighthouse that stood sentinel at the easternmost edge of the state park.

"Is the lighthouse manned?" John asked.

Audrey shook her head. "No. The lighthouse became automated in the late 1980s—"

"And the park closed in mid-October for the winter," Paulson interjected. "So basically, were alone out here without internet or cell service."

"There's a satellite phone in the watch room," Audrey assured him through gritted teeth. His whining was getting on her nerves. "The mayor insisted on putting one in several years ago when the automated system failed during a storm. That way if it ever fails again or needs to be serviced and the lighthouse has to be manned, there's a way to communicate with the outside world."

Inside the lighthouse, they made their way to the watch room. The glow from the lantern beam reflected off the oblong windows encasing the watch room. Audrey stared out at the dark night beyond and thanked God they'd made it safely.

Paulson dropped his duffel in the middle of the room. "The sheriff said to bring you a change of clothes." He tugged open the drawstring top and pulled out several things. "I grabbed some of my brother's things he'd left in our spare room when he last visited. You're about his size." Paulson then made a beeline for the satellite phone set up in the corner. "I'm going to let the sheriff know what's happened."

John snatched up the clothes Paulson had provided before moving to stand beside Audrey. "You okay?"

Turning to stare into his dark eyes, she felt the need to share her thoughts. "Just thanking God we made it here in one piece. I'll admit I was a bit nervous out there."

One side of his mouth lifted in a lopsided grin. "Only a bit? I was downright petrified."

She cocked one eyebrow, and a smile tugged at the corner of her mouth. Her hair had come loose from the clip in the back during their hike. Long tendrils curled over the collar of her uniform and tickled her neck. She pushed a strand back. "Oh? So you doubted me? But I got us here safely."

He reached up to lay claim to a lock of blond hair, rubbing the silky strands between his fingers. "Yes, you did. And very expertly, at that."

His praise softened something inside her. She mentally scrambled to reclaim her professional detachment, but apparently it was hiding behind tender affection.

John glanced at Paulson, who had his back to them. Then he tugged her close and leaned toward her but stilled with just a few inches between them. allowing her the opportunity to step away, to put a stop to what was about to happen.

Appreciation and attraction heated her skin. She knew the right thing to do would to be step back, create space between them, both physically and emotionally, but her feet stayed rooted to the ground. Longing welled from deep inside her, and she found she wanted, needed his kiss.

"Hey, guys." Paulson's voice broke through the moment. "The sheriff has some news you might want to hear."

Irritated by the interruption, and without breaking eye contact with John, Audrey asked, "What is it?"

"Sheriff knows John's real name."

The words dispersed the intimacy of the moment.

John sucked in a breath. Audrey felt his anticipation and his dread in her gut. Finally they would find out who he was and hopefully why someone wanted to kill him.

SEVEN

"Yes, sir," Paulson said into the phone. "I'll let them know." He hung up.

Audrey's gaze jerked away from John, and her jaw dropped. She couldn't believe Paulson had dropped the bomb that the sheriff knew John's identity and then disconnected without letting her or John talk to the sheriff. "Wait! Why did you hang up?" She rushed across the room to grab the phone from Paulson. "What did the sheriff say?"

John stalked closer, his jaw set in a tight line. His dark eyes bored holes into Paulson. So different from the man who moments ago had nearly kissed her. She swallowed back the disappointment at being interrupted, even though she knew kissing John would have been a huge, colossal mistake. She couldn't let herself be taken in by his charm and good looks, even though there was more to him than that.

He'd trusted her when he had no reason to. He'd shown her respect and consideration. He was struggling in a difficult situation yet had shown concern for others. She admitted to herself she liked him.

However, she had to keep an emotional distance. Once he discovered who he was and where he belonged, he'd leave Calico Bay behind, while her life was rooted here.

Letting herself become attached would only set her up for heartbreak, both personally and professionally. She had to keep her eye on the future, on her goal of one day being sheriff. The town deserved a leader that could keep her emotions in check.

"Hey, don't get mad at me." Paulson held up his hands, palms out. "Sheriff said he received a call from someone in the Canadian government." He glanced at John. "They're sending people here."

"What kind of people?" Officers to take John into custody? The thought made her blood run cold.

"Did he give you my name?" John asked in a razor-sharp tone that sent a shiver down Audrey's spine. His fingers flexed around the bundle of clothes in his hands.

Paulson nodded eagerly. "Nathanial Longhorn. Ring any bells?"

Audrey held her breath. John's blank expression didn't bode well.

Slowly he shook his head. "No. Did he tell you anything else? Do I have a family?"

Paulson shook his head. "Sheriff said no wife, no kids."

That was good, wasn't it? He turned on his heel and paced back to the window overlooking the ocean.

Directly above them, up a ten-rung metal ladder, was the lantern room, where the electrical, nonrotating lighthouse signal was housed. It blinked every two seconds, throwing a beam of light fifteen nautical miles over the water, warning of the rocky jut of land they stood on.

Empathy engulfed her. She couldn't imagine the frustration of not knowing who he was or his past. She wanted to go to him, wrap her arms around him and tell him it would be all right. But she doubted he'd believe her. Not to mention that would be so inappropriate.

Something bad had happened to this man. Someone

was still trying to kill him. And despite others' misgivings, she felt deep inside that he was a good man. A man who deserved her protection.

She couldn't be wrong about him. Could she? She sent up a silent prayer asking God to make the truth known. If she were proven wrong, then so be it, but until then she would continue to believe in him and hope for the best.

"Sheriff requested we head to the station first thing in the morning and he'll give you all the details," Paulson continued. "He's also got Harrison and Dietrich out patrolling, looking for the SUV."

Audrey cradled the phone, tempted to call the sheriff back, but she knew her great-uncle liked to do things in person. If he'd wanted to discuss John—er, Nathanial—over the phone, he would have. She set the phone aside. "I guess we have to exercise some patience. Morning will come soon enough."

She walked to Nathanial's side and stared at his proud profile. His jaw worked. Most likely gnashing his teeth with irritation at having to wait to learn more about himself. "I'm sorry you don't recognize your name."

His lips twisted. "Not your fault. It's strange, you know. When I apply the name *Nathanial* to myself, it feels tight in my brain." He grimaced. "I'm not sure how to explain."

"Maybe it's part of whatever your mind is protecting you from. You know—" she dropped her voice an octave "—the betrayal."

He blew out a breath. "Yeah. I guess." He turned to face her. His dark, troubled eyes searched her face. "Thank you."

Surprise bloomed in her chest. "For what?"

"Saving my life. Keeping me safe. I have the strangest feeling that I should be the one protecting you."

She smiled and put her hand on his arm. His muscles bunched beneath her palm. "I'm not the one in danger."

"Except that when you're with me, you are," he countered.

She squeezed his arm. "Part of the job." She removed her hand. "Come with me to the visitors' center. There's a restroom where you can change your clothes. And I'll see if I can find us some food, since we skipped dinner."

He extended his hand, indicating she go first. "Lead the way."

She took him down an interior spiral staircase and opened the door to an attached portion of the building with a key on her key ring. "This once was the lighthouse keeper's quarters but was renovated into a visitors' center and museum. The US Coast Guard had a station here back in the day. When they abandoned the property, the Yeaton family took it over and made the old station into rental property, which is where we would have been staying had our enemies in the black SUV not followed us." She pointed to the left. "Restrooms are there."

"Why do you have keys to the lighthouse?" he asked.

"My great-great-great-grandmother was related to Hopley Yeaton, a naval captain in the late 1700s. He was considered to be the father of the US Coast Guard. The lighthouse association wanted me on the board because of the relation, and they gave me a set of keys."

"Not only are you beautiful, you're American royalty," he commented with a gleam of interest in his eyes.

A heated flush rose up her neck and settled in her cheeks. He was so smooth with his compliments. If she weren't careful, she'd find herself following through on the promise of a kiss. "I'm going to go look for some food."

His soft laugh followed her into the store part of the visitors' center. She gathered bags of trail mix, beef jerky and bottles of water. She wrote out an IOU and set it on the counter. In the spring when the center reopened, she'd settle up. It wasn't like anyone wouldn't know where to find her.

"Any chance there's a razor around?" Nathanial stepped into the store wearing the change of clothes provided by Paulson.

He looked so different in well-worn jeans that looked like they were tailor-made for his long, lean legs and trim waist. A plaid flannel shirt in Christmas colors stretched across his broad shoulders. He'd rolled the sleeves up to reveal muscled forearms. He'd dampened his hair and slicked it back with his fingers. He rubbed a hand over his stubbled jaw, and her own fingers curled with the yearning to do the same.

"Sorry, no." Normally she didn't go in for the scruffy look, but on him it worked well. "Tomorrow when we go back into town, we can hit the mercantile."

He eyed her bounty. "You found a feast." She handed him a couple bags of trail mix and a bottle of water.

"It's not fancy but will have to do." They took the stairs to the watchtower.

Paulson was on the outside catwalk. When he saw them he came inside. He rubbed his arms and shivered. "It's definitely going to snow again soon. I hope we don't get stuck here."

"See anything out there?" Audrey asked. There was no way the men in the SUV would just give up. She figured they were waiting for daylight before resuming their hunt for Nathanial. At least she hoped that was the case.

If they found the gravel road to the trailhead, they could hike in and stage an assault. But that could happen anywhere. At least here in the lighthouse, they had the advantage of a high viewpoint and could see them coming.

"No. It's dark and quiet out there," Paulson replied as he accepted the bottle of water she offered him. "I found a pile of blankets in the closet. I'll grab a couple and head downstairs to watch the door."

She handed him a stick of beef jerky and a bag of trail mix. "I can take the first watch."

"Not necessary," Paulson said, taking the offered treats, and grabbed two blankets from the pile on the floor. "We can trade off in a few hours."

There was something in his tone that grated on her nerves and led her to think he wouldn't make the trade out of some chivalrous need to protect the female. For half a second she contemplated arguing with him and demanding she take the first watch, but then she decided it wasn't worth the aggravation. She'd set her watch alarm and relieve him from guard duty whether he wanted her to or not.

Nathanial found a chair and dragged it to the center of the room. "Do you have cuffs on you?"

She turned to face him. "Excuse me?"

"Your boss was right to put me in a cell," he stated. He sat and placed his hands on the armrests of the chair. "We don't know my story. The people coming to claim me could very well be taking me to prison."

"No." She wouldn't accept that despite the validity in his words. "If the sheriff thought you were a threat to me and Paulson, he wouldn't have called—he'd have shown up and taken you into his custody."

"Why do you believe in me?" He tilted his head and stared at her with curiosity gleaming in his dark eyes.

She stepped closer. "My grandmother always told me I had a good sense of people. The sheriff says it's what makes me good at my job." Her mouth twisted wryly. "It just seems to be in my love life that my judgment fails." Oh, brother. Had she just said that out loud? Embarrassment sent a heated flush through her. Maybe he'd let the admission slip by without comment.

He reached out and took her hand. "Tell me."

She tried to disengage from his grasp, but he held firm. His thumb made little circles on her palm, igniting a maelstrom of tingles to career through her. Totally distracting her. "What?"

He rose, pulling her closer, trapping her hand against his chest. Warmth infused her, chasing away the chill of the lighthouse. "Tell me about the man who made you so shy of relationships."

She had to tilt her head back to meet his gaze. She wasn't used to having to do that. More often than not, she was taller than the men in her life. The look in his eyes enthralled her. Her breath caught in her chest and held. She didn't want to think about Kyle, much less talk about him. She licked her lips. Nathanial's gaze tracked the movement. Her insides quivered. "What makes you think there was someone?"

His mouth curved. "I may not remember my name or my past, but I can read you. You're uncomfortable with compliments, which suggests you don't trust flattering words. You have a chip on your shoulder about being regarded as an equal by your peers and your boss that tells me you've had to prove yourself over and over again. And you keep an emotional barrier up." He grinned. "Plus, my innate charm seems to offend you."

His words dug into wounds she'd thought she'd kept hidden. She lifted her chin. "I'm sure everything you just said could apply to most women in my position. And it isn't so much offense I feel at your charm. I just distrust it."

He conceded her point by inclining his head. "Probably. And you're wise to distrust charm until you're certain it's genuine." A wry expression spread over his handsome face. "It takes a strong and intelligent woman to enter a field that has traditionally been dominated by men. And you, Deputy Audrey Martin, are a strong and intelligent woman."

If he only knew. Shame and guilt rushed in to kick her in the gut. She dropped her gaze and once again tried to put distance between them. He lifted her hand to kiss her knuckles, effectively stopping her in her tracks.

She swallowed and watched his nicely formed lips place feather-like touches against her skin. He was torturing her without inflicting pain. Instead, he stirred yearnings deep in her heart.

Yearnings for someone to make her feel special. Someone whom she could be herself with, not always have to be brave and tough. Someone who would be true, genuine.

She'd be foolish to look for that with this man. There was too much unknown about him. And she needed to remember what she really wanted in life—to be sheriff. Not some lovesick, wimpy woman trailing after a man with no memory.

"I would never purposely hurt you," he said softly, as if he could read her mind. "That's why I think you need to cuff me to the chair and stay far away from me."

Probably good advice. But every instinct rebelled at the thought. "Not happening. If you want to talk, we can talk. But I'm not chaining you to a chair without a reason."

This time when she tugged on her hand, he released her. She moved to the pile of blankets. She wrapped one around her shoulders and then handed him one. He did the same. They sat on the floor with their backs propped up against the wall. They munched on trail mix and beef jerky.

"So," he finally said. "Spill."

Her jaw clenched. Her teeth sank into an almond. Her mouth went dry. She took a swig of water, debating how and what to say. "It's not a big deal," she said, hoping to play nonchalant. "I fell in a love with a jerk. We broke up. I've been gun-shy of romance ever since. End of story."

"I doubt that. What made him a jerk?"

"He was a player. Had me on a string along with several other women. He'd led me to believe I was special, that he cared about me." She let out a mirthless laugh. "I should have known better. I did know better, but I was blinded by his charm. He'd talked me into setting aside my values and faith with empty promises of forever."

"Ouch. How did it end?"

She grimaced, remembering the scene she'd made. "I broke it off. In the quad. Very loudly."

Nathanial chuckled. "Good for you. You don't strike me as the type to quietly slip away. You're a woman of action."

That made her smile. "I haven't seen him since that day I told him we were through, but I heard he went on to Georgetown and became a lawyer."

"I'd make a crack about lawyers, but I don't believe in generalizations," he said. "Not all lawyers, just like not all men, are made from the same cloth."

What cloth was he made from, she wondered.

"And you haven't dated since the jerk?"

She shrugged. "A few dates. Nothing serious." No one had made her heart beat faster. But Nathanial did. She didn't understand her attraction to him. Was it the allure of mystery surrounding his loss of memory? Or was he the one her mother had always said would come along and make her rethink her life? She frowned at that thought. She had no intention of rethinking her path.

"What's Sean's story?"

She tucked in her chin at the sudden change in topic. Did he know about Sean's crush on her? "What do you mean?"

"I saw his prosthetic."

Her heart thumped with sadness and pride for the young man she thought of as a brother. "Afghanistan. Four years ago. His unit was ambushed by Taliban insurgents."

"That's rough."

"Yeah. He was a combat medic." She couldn't keep the bitter taste of anger out of her tone. "He was there to help others."

"He was also a soldier," Nathanial stated quietly.

"Yes. He earned his Combat Medical Badge for providing care under fire. From what I've heard, he helped others while he was injured himself." She swallowed past the lump in her throat. "He's a hero."

"It must have been hard for him to return to this quiet community after the chaos of war."

"He had a hard time adjusting at first," she admitted. "Watching him come to terms with his loss was difficult for everyone. The town pulled together, sent him back to school to become a civilian paramedic and bought the ambulance."

Nathanial winced. "Which was destroyed because of me."

"No, it was destroyed because criminals tried to kill you. The insurance will get Sean another ambulance."

"He has a crush on you."

Biting back a groan, she popped a handful of trail mix into her mouth and chewed, giving herself time to formulate an answer to a complicated situation. After she took another drink of water, she said, "He's the younger brother of one of my childhood best friends. I couldn't... I mean, he's like the little brother I never had."

"Ah. Good."

She arched an eyebrow. "Good?" She turned to face him

fully. Though shadows played over his features, there was no mistaking the intensity in his expression.

"I wasn't sure if you and he…" Nathanial's mouth lifted at the corner. "I was hoping you weren't involved with him."

Her pulse kicked up. "Why?"

"Because then I'd feel guilty for kissing you."

"But you haven't kissed me."

"You're right, we were interrupted."

He touched her cheek, his fingers trailing across her skin. She sucked in a quick breath. Her heart hammered. She was torn between wanting him to kiss her and wanting, needing, to keep a distance. He lowered his head, once again pausing, letting her make the final decision.

So many conflicting thoughts swirled in her head. She was setting herself up for hurt. She was curious, wanting to know what it would feel like to kiss this man. She was supposed to be protecting him, not forming some romantic attachment. But would one kiss qualify as an attachment? One kiss couldn't hurt anything, could it?

Her mind flashed to Kyle. To the seduction he'd laid on her, beguiling her into believing that taking one step wouldn't lead to another and another, until he'd led her down a path that had left her filled with guilt and shame. And anger when he'd shown his true colors.

She put her fingers against Nathanial's lips. The warmth of his mouth flowed through her, making her hesitate. But she forged ahead, knowing she was making the right choice. "I can't. This isn't going to happen."

Disappointment shone in the dark depths of his eyes, but he nodded, retreating from her both physically and emotionally. It was like an invisible barrier had gone up between them. She didn't like it but had no idea what to do about it, either.

He settled his head against the wall. "We should get some rest. Tomorrow you won't have to worry about me anymore. I'll become someone else's problem."

You're not a problem, she wanted to tell him. But she held her tongue. And he was wrong. She'd continue to worry about him as long as someone was out to kill him.

EIGHT

The next morning, after dropping Paulson off at his house, Nathanial and Audrey headed to the sheriff's station and parked at the curb outside. Nathanial gripped the interior door handle of Audrey's bright blue muscle car. A muscle car. Go figure. The woman was full of surprises.

Last night when they'd climbed into the Mustang, he'd thought the sweet ride too much car for the beautiful deputy, but the way she'd outmaneuvered their pursuers had made it clear that the woman knew how to drive. And was skilled. He'd been impressed and attracted. He had a strong feeling he'd never met anyone like Audrey. But then again, how would he know? His brain wasn't cooperating.

Learning his name was Nathanial Longhorn had been surreal. The name fit like a too-small glove, making his mind and heart anxious. He'd tried to explain the sensation to Audrey, but how did he explain something he didn't understand?

Like his attraction to the pretty blonde. Well, okay, that he could understand. What man in his right mind—or not right, as the case might be with him—wouldn't be attracted to a tall, curvy, beautiful woman?

But it was more than her looks. She was special on the inside, too. Resourceful. Calm in the face of danger.

Protective but not overbearing. And that chip she carried on her shoulder was so obvious, yet she tried not to let it rule her.

He'd noticed that she hadn't liked it when Paulson had taken the first watch last night. She'd wanted to prove she was up to the task. There was no question in Nathanial's mind that she was capable, and he was thankful she'd chosen to swallow her need to take action. He'd been able to spend more time with her, and she'd opened up to him, trusting him with the story of her past romantic relationship. Though he had a feeling there was more to the story, he hadn't pushed. Instead...

His hand flexed on the door handle.

He'd made a fool of himself. He'd allowed his attraction and a deep-seated yearning for connection to overtake his common sense. He'd made a pass at her and been rebuffed.

As he should have been. He had no business starting something with the lovely Audrey when he had no idea why someone was trying to kill him.

Once they stepped inside the sheriff's station, she would no longer be in danger because of him.

He would accept whatever awaited him inside the brick building, despite the constriction in his lungs and the pounding in his head. By the grace of God above he would leave Audrey and Calico Bay behind, taking with him the danger that lurked in the shadows.

From the driver's seat, Audrey asked, "Are you nervous?"

Nathanial slanted her a glance. No doubt she was wondering why he was hesitating. Maybe he was a coward at heart. Something inside rebelled at the thought, but he couldn't shake the dread crimping his shoulder muscles and making his breathing labored. Forcing air into his lungs, he gave her a rueful twist of his lips and admitted, "Yeah, I am."

She reached across the center console and touched his arm, her hand warm against his skin exposed by the rolled-up sleeve of the plaid flannel shirt he wore. "It's understandable. But I'm here, and I'm not going to let anything bad happen to you."

The tightness around his mind and heart eased a fraction. He covered her hand with his. He was amazed by her dedication to him. She had no reason to believe in him. For all they knew, he would be taken into custody by the Canadian government and hauled away for crimes he couldn't remember.

His throat closed. He blinked back the emotions choking him and managed to say, "I appreciate your support. Whatever happens, I hope you know that you have been a bright spot in an otherwise bleak existence."

The corners of her mouth lifted slightly. "Melodrama much?"

He chuckled. "I guess so."

She gave his arm a squeeze before withdrawing her hand and opening her door. "Come on. Better to get this over with quickly rather than drawing it out."

He liked her pragmatic outlook. He rolled his shoulders, took a deep breath and popped the door open. He stepped out into the brisk morning air. He glanced up and down the street, studying the vehicles, looking for the SUV and the men inside.

Reflexively his gaze lifted. He wasn't sure what instinct made him search the rooftops of the buildings stretching along the main road of town.

Something glinted in the morning sunlight.

A jolt of adrenaline kick-started his pulse. He grabbed Audrey and yanked her to the sidewalk. A fraction of a second later, a *crack* split the air. He dived over her, covering her with his body. A bullet slammed into the cement inches from his head. Bits of concrete stung his flesh. The noise stunned his ears.

"Get off me!" Audrey yelled.

He rolled toward the cover of the car, taking her with him as a barrage of gunfire followed in their wake. They landed with a thud against the back passenger door. He scooted them over to use the tire for extra cover.

Audrey scrambled to a squat and drew her sidearm. "Where's the shooter?"

"Two blocks up. Southeast corner." His hand flexed with the need to return fire.

The sheriff and four other men rushed out of the station, each with a gun in hand. Nathanial glimpsed gold badges on belts beneath various types of jackets. He didn't have time to study the men as Audrey waved them back.

"Shooter," she called out. "Southeast corner of the bank."

Sheriff Crump nodded and disappeared inside. The four strangers spread out in a tactical pattern with weapons drawn. They took cover behind bushes and poles. Clearly these were the men sent to retrieve him. One man, tall and well-dressed in a long wool coat over slacks and a dress shirt and tie, motioned for him and Audrey to come to the safety of the station. He had dark hair swept back from a hard-edged face.

"We'll cover you," he called out.

Nathanial shared a quick glance with Audrey.

"You go," he told her. "You're not the target."

Her gaze narrowed, and her jaw firmed. "I'm not leaving you. We go together."

The stubborn resolve in her blue eyes let him know arguing with her was futile. He gave one sharp nod. She scrambled to his other side—the side that put her in the direct line of the shooter. Tension vibrated through his body. A siren rent the air. Obviously the sheriff had called for reinforcements.

She put her hand on his shoulder. "Move with me."

Hating the vulnerable feeling stealing over him, he had no choice but to let her do her job. "Let's go."

They hurried across the expanse of sidewalk. The men closed ranks behind them, covering their flank. Nathanial braced himself for another round of gunfire that never came. They made it inside the building, and the sheriff hustled them out of the lobby and into the bull pen where the deputies had their desks.

"Get down," the sheriff instructed.

Nathanial crouched beside Audrey behind a thick metal desk.

The men spread out, covering windows, while the one who'd taken the lead stayed near the doorway. The sheriff's radio crackled.

"Sheriff." Deputy Harrison's voice echoed in the station. "Shooter escaped. Found spent shell casings, but nothing else."

"Copy," the sheriff said. "Stay put. Keep alert. I'll send Lindsey and her team over."

"Lindsey? Team?" Nathanial asked Audrey.

She rose and holstered her weapon. "The county's forensic specialists."

He stood and faced the congregated men. The leader leveled Nathanial with an intense, searching stare. Not that the other three men's gazes weren't equal in intensity, but for some reason this man's eyes provoked an odd sensation of alertness within Nathanial.

Disconcerted by the response, Nathanial studied the other men. They ranged in age from roughly twenties to somewhere in their thirties. He mentally shrugged. It was hard to tell with intense men like these. They held themselves with an air of authority that no one could miss. They were dressed in civilian clothes, so Nathanial hadn't a clue which branch of the Canadian government they worked for.

Audrey stepped to his side, silently offering her support, drawing the men's attention. He didn't like the way they assessed her with both curiosity and wariness. He had the strangest urge to slip an arm around her in a show of possession. He wanted to stake his claim on Audrey and make it clear she was off-limits.

He clenched his jaw. That was so out of left field and not going to happen. She'd been very direct that she wasn't interested. And he shouldn't be, either.

He cleared his throat, drawing the men's focus back to him. "You may have heard my memories before waking on the beach here in Calico Bay are gone."

The man nearest him nodded. "We've heard. The doctor says retrograde amnesia. Your memory could return at any time."

Surprise flickered through Nathanial. They'd discussed his condition with Dr. Martin. "I've been told my name is Nathanial Longhorn. But that doesn't tell me who I am or why someone wants me dead."

The bigger of the four men stepped forward. "We can fill in some of the first part but not the latter." There was sympathy and wariness in his hazel eyes.

Frustration mingled with relief. "Then tell me what you can. Starting with who you are."

The big man's mouth twitched. He stuck out his hand. "Inspector Drew Kelley with the Royal Canadian Mounted Police."

Nathanial grasped his hand. "Nice to meet you."

"I'm Luke Wellborn," the youngest of the group said

as he moved forward with his hand out. He was slighter in frame than the others, with intelligent gray eyes and a firm grip. "US Border Patrol."

The other man hung back. There was no mistaking the anger in the man's blue gaze as he tipped his chin. "Chase Smith, ATF."

The acronym for the United States Bureau of Alcohol, Tobacco, Firearms and Explosives slammed into Nathanial. American and Canadian law enforcement. What did that mean?

"You really don't remember anything?" Chase asked.

Studying the other man, Nathanial tried to find some spark of recognition and failed. He shook his head. "No. Nothing."

By the derisive curl of Chase's lip, Nathanial had no problem discerning the guy didn't believe him. What were RCMP, USBP and ATF doing here? Nathanial turned his focus on the last man in the group. The one he'd pegged as the leader. There was something in the man's expression that tugged at Nathanial, making him want to remember, but the more he probed his mind, the more his head throbbed.

"Blake Fallon, ICE."

"Immigration and Customs Enforcement," Nathanial said beneath his breath.

Blake moved closer, his dark eyes going to the place on Nathanial's head that still bore the mark of the blow he'd sustained prior to washing ashore on the beach. "What is the last thing you *do* remember?"

"I told you," Nathanial said. "Nothing of my life before waking up in the hospital. I didn't know my name until you gave it to the sheriff." He looked at Drew. "You said you could fill me in on who I am. How do I know my name really is Nathanial?"

Blake withdrew a black wallet from the inside pocket of his long wool coat. "Here. This belongs to you."

Mouth turning to cotton, Nathanial accepted the offered item. The soft leather felt strange in his hand. He flipped it open. On one side was a gold badge with the Canada Border Services Agency emblem, and the other held a driver's license issued in Saskatchewan, Canada, with his photo, name and stats. So many questions ran through his head. He was Canadian? Why did an ICE agent have his wallet? What waited for him at the address on the driver's license? The pounding in his head intensified, making him wince. He passed the wallet over to Audrey.

"I knew it," she said beneath her breath. "I knew you were one of the good guys."

He wanted to believe she was right. Was she? "I'm a border officer?"

"For several years," Drew said. "A good one, too."

Pressure built behind his eyes. "Why does it take four federal agencies from two countries to come for me?"

"You're one of us," Blake said. "We are all part of a cross-border task force. We've been working together for four years."

"Task force." The words reverberated through his brain, setting off a pinging of pain that made him clutch his head for fear his skull would crack open. The room dimmed. He could feel his legs weaken. Blindly he reached for Audrey. He grasped the sleeve of her jacket.

Her strong hand gripped his shoulders. "Nathanial." His name sounded foreign on her lips. "What is it? What can I do to help?"

Audrey's soothing voice brought him back from the edge. He fought the pain, found strength in her touch, her presence. He focused his gaze on her concerned face, letting the sight of her ground him, calm him. It didn't make sense that this woman, whom he barely knew, should be the one to anchor him, rather than these men he apparently worked closely with.

"Here, sit." Blake dragged a chair to him. "The doctor said you'd been having headaches."

Bracing his feet apart, Nathanial remained standing. He gave Audrey a nod to let her know it was okay for her to let go of him. She removed her hands from his shoulders but stayed glued to his side. To Blake, Nathanial said, "What happened? How did I end up on a beach in Maine?"

Blake ran his fingers through his brown hair. "We don't know."

"We were in the middle of a mission when you went rogue," Chase said, his voice hard.

"We don't know that he went rogue," Drew interjected with a tone of warning.

Chase's mouth set in a firm line, and he spun away to stare out the station window.

A shudder of dread rippled through Nathanial. "What was the mission?"

"To take down a known gunrunner operating out of Saint John Harbour, New Brunswick," Blake supplied. "We had good intel that a shipment had been smuggled over from the States."

"You were on overwatch," Drew told him.

Nathanial winced as a fresh sliver of pain pierced through his brain. "I don't know what that is."

Chase made a disgruntled sound. Nathanial wondered if they'd been enemies before, or was his animosity due to his belief that Nathanial had gone rogue? The thought that he'd abandoned his post willingly left him feeling hollow inside.

"You're an expert marksman," Blake said.

"And you're lethal with a knife," Luke, the USBP agent, chimed in.

Nathanial absorbed their pronouncements, but the words held no relevance for him. Yet…hadn't he longed to feel the weight of a weapon in his hand? Now at least he knew why. But he couldn't visualize himself with a gun or a blade.

"What happened on that day?" Audrey asked. "I take it from your comments Nathanial disappeared."

"Yes." Blake's dark gaze focused on Audrey for a moment. Nathanial recognized the gleam of speculation there before Blake turned his gaze on him. Nathanial wasn't prepared for the bleak sadness flooding the man's expression. "You were on the roof with an assault rifle. Your job was to scout the area and to keep those on the ground informed of any potential threats."

Nathanial's stomach dropped. He had a horrible feeling that he'd failed. Purposely? "I left my post?"

A tense moment of silence met his question. Finally Blake gave a short nod. "Yes. One moment you were on the com device in my ear telling me to hold on. Then static."

"We sent men to the roof to see what happened," Drew said. "They found your rifle, com devices and your Becker Necker lying abandoned."

Nathanial wasn't sure what a Becker Necker was, so he glanced at Audrey to see if she did.

"A combat knife made by the US company Ka-Bar," she answered his unspoken question. Then she turned her sharp-eyed gaze on Blake. "What's a Canada Border Services officer doing carrying a US-made military knife?"

"It was a gift," Blake replied. A muscle jumped in his jaw, as if he were struggling to contain some emotion.

Had the knife been a present from a woman? Nathanial

hadn't yet asked if there was someone in his life waiting for him. His chest ached thinking about it.

"I have one, too," Drew interjected. "Which is why I know you didn't leave that roof of your own free will. You wouldn't have left that behind."

Nathanial's gaze bounced between the two men. "Who was the gift from?"

Drew looked at Blake.

Blake swallowed. "From me. It was a groomsman gift."

"I was in your wedding." Nathanial's voice sounded strangled to his own ears. Obviously they'd been good friends. His heart ached. *Why, Lord, can't I remember these men?*

"You were my best man," Blake added in a rough voice.

Best friends.

He heard Audrey's sharp intake of breath. A wave of frustration hit him, making his stomach roil and his heart feel crushed. He tried to remember, to call up memories of a happy period in his life. But there was nothing but a black abyss that threatened to swallow him whole.

As if sensing the turmoil going on inside him, Audrey slipped her hand into his. He took comfort from her touch, her steady presence.

"Enough with the bro-fest." Chase whirled from the window and stalked toward him.

Nathanial tensed. Drew made a move to intercept Chase, but the ATF agent held up his hand and shook his head before he returned his attention to Nathanial. The barely suppressed fury wasn't as surprising as the pain underlining the more volatile emotion.

"We came here to uncover the truth." Chase's tone was ragged, haunted. "My men deserve that."

Everything inside Nathanial froze. "What aren't you telling me?"

Nathanial looked to Blake. The grimness in his eyes didn't bode well. A lump of dread lodged in Nathanial's throat. A heavy, oppressive weight bore down on him. He focused back on Chase. The world narrowed to where he could see only the other man's blue eyes.

"Two of my men died because you left your post."

NINE

The air rushed out of Audrey's lungs. Warmth from the sheriff's station's heater had sweat breaking out on her skin beneath the heavy weight of her uniform vest. The declaration by the man named Chase echoed in her head. Men had died because Nathanial hadn't been there to warn them of an attack.

Her gaze swept over the other men, hoping for some sign of denial, but the anguish in each man's eyes told the truth. Her heart twisted with empathy. Losing a comrade in arms was never easy. That these men blamed Nathanial sent a shiver across her nape. She wanted to defend him, tell them he would never do what they were accusing him of, yet did she really know what he would or wouldn't do?

Was she letting her heart rule over her head?

She knew next to nothing about this man, yet she couldn't shake the deep, instinctive reaction that kept her glued to his side. She wouldn't condemn him without proof. But she'd better keep her heart in check. Letting herself become attached to this man wasn't wise, because if her gut was wrong, she'd not only be embarrassed and in potential danger but she risked having her heart bruised again. A fate she wanted to avoid at all costs.

Standing beside her, Nathanial swayed. For a moment

she thought he was going down. She reached out to steady him as he sank onto the chair the ICE agent, Blake, had previously offered him.

Nathanial put his head into his hands. "I wish I could remember what happened."

The tortured tone of his voice tugged at her heart. She met Blake's gaze. "He was hit over the head and thrown into the sea. We found a tracking device embedded in his boot heel. That has to mean he wasn't involved, right?"

Blake's eyes widened, and he shared a glance with the Mountie. "Someone took him out of commission."

"But the question is who," Drew stated.

Luke Wellborn, the US Border Patrol agent, had been hanging back but now stepped forward, his boyish face pale. "One of Kosloff's men."

The AFT agent, Chase, rubbed his jaw. "Or one of ours," he stated grimly. "There's no way Kosloff knew we were there unless a mole told him. But whether Officer Longhorn was involved or not is still up for debate. We don't know that he was attacked. He could have easily slipped, hit his head and fallen into the ocean. After giving up my men's location."

"Then how do you explain someone trying to kill him? Repeatedly," Audrey shot back.

"There's no honor among bad guys." Chase shrugged. "He may have outlived his usefulness."

"I don't believe that," Blake said. "I know Nathanial. He would never betray his country or the team."

Did they forget he was sitting there? She didn't like that they talked about John, er, Nathanial—it was weird to be calling him by a different name now— so callously. Yet he couldn't defend himself, because he didn't know the truth. His mind refused to cooperate. It was maddening and frightful at the same time.

"I agree," Drew said. "I trust Nathanial."

"We'll let the director make the determination of his guilt or not," Chase said. He fixed his gaze on Nathanial. "We're taking you to the IBETs headquarters."

Nathanial lifted his head. "Which is where?"

"Washington, DC." Blake moved closer and put a hand on Nathanial's shoulder. "Don't worry, we'll keep you safe." Blake glanced at her. "Thank you, Deputy. We'll take it from here."

For some reason his assurance didn't alleviate the worry in Audrey's gut. She couldn't just let go of the case, not to mention she didn't quite trust these men. It was her job to protect her community, to protect this man and to do her job she needed to uncover the truth.

And the only way she would be able to discover what was really going on was if she stuck close to Nathanial. She was about to tell the ICE man that when Nathanial jerked to his feet.

"No. I'm not going with you," he said. The panic in his dark eyes wrenched at her heart. "I don't know you. You say I do, but I don't remember you, and I'm supposed to just trust you?"

She couldn't stop herself from putting her hand on his arm, offering him some comfort.

His gaze jerked to her and held for a long moment, and then he took a shuddering breath. His expression clearing, his jaw hardened. "I have to go with them."

Narrowing her gaze, she protested, "No, you don't. You're in my custody. I'm not ready to release you."

His eyes softened before shuttering, closing off his emotions. "It's time. I've put you in enough danger."

Her back teeth slammed together as she curbed the jolt of disbelief and anger that reared up. If he thought he was going to sacrifice his safety by going with these men that he'd already admitted he didn't know or trust because of some misguided sense of chivalry, he had another thing coming. She didn't need anyone protecting her. She was capable of protecting herself and him. "If you go, I go."

He blinked and tucked his chin. "I can't ask that of you."

She arched an eyebrow. "You're not. And hear me clearly, I'm not asking for your permission, either."

A small smile curved his lips. "You're a force to be reckoned with, Deputy Martin."

Heat crept up her neck, but she held his gaze. "Yes. And don't forget it."

He laughed at that. "I wouldn't dream of it."

"Then that's settled," Sheriff Crump said, stepping into the conversation. "Deputy Martin will escort Officer Longhorn to Washington, DC, for his debriefing with Director Moore."

All four federal agents stared at the sheriff.

Blake canted his head. "How did…"

The sheriff's smile wasn't exactly smug, but Audrey had seen that look on her great-uncle's face before. He'd already checked out these men. She wasn't surprised. Great-uncle David wasn't a pushover. And he was thorough. She hoped to be just like him when she became sheriff.

"The minute you contacted me, Agent Fallon, I was on the phone with Homeland Security," the sheriff said, confirming Audrey's thoughts. "I'm sure Director Moore will appreciate the extra security for your team."

The looks on the men's faces said they sure didn't appreciate it, but she didn't care. She was going to stick close to Nathanial. She couldn't deny the prospect pleased her more than it should. Though she had a feeling keeping her heart safe from unexpected emotions stirred by Nathanial might prove to be a harder proposition than finding the truth about what had happened to him.

* * *

When they touched down in Washington, DC, they were whisked away from Reagan National Airport in black SUVs. Nathanial and Audrey were in the second vehicle with ICE agent Blake Fallon driving and RCMP inspector Drew Kelley in the front passenger seat. Up ahead in another identical Suburban, the ATF agent Chase Smith and US Border Patrol agent Luke Wellborn led the way through the late-afternoon metro-area traffic.

Snow covered the ground and piled at the curbs, where snowplows had pushed back the white powder and sprinkled salt on the asphalt to make the roads passable. Strings of white lights clung to the streetlamps and trees lining the avenues. Pedestrians, bundled beneath heavy coats and scarves, made their way along the sidewalks.

From the back passenger seat of the second SUV, Nathanial stared out the side window at the many passing monuments and statues memorializing the United States of America. He could name the monolithic Washington Monument bathed in white lights, but he didn't know how he knew its name or whether he'd seen it before. He recognized the Lincoln Memorial and the White House. But putting labels to the structures was as far as his memory allowed.

His gaze moved to the brightly lit, large evergreen Christmas tree located south of the White House as a headache born of frustration and tension pounded at his temples and tightened the muscles of his neck and shoulders. *Merry Christmas.* He rolled his shoulders and glanced at his seatmate.

Audrey peered through the windows with an avid expression of awe.

"You've never been to the nation's capital before?" he asked.

She smiled at him, and his heart thumped in his chest. She had a great smile, and it eased some of his anxiety. There was something about this woman that calmed his nerves. He figured there was some psychological mumbo jumbo that could explain his reaction to her.

She snook her head, and he caught a whiff of her vanilla-scented perfume. "I've always wanted to come here for vacation. There's so much to see."

Before leaving Calico Bay, she'd changed into civilian clothes when she'd hurried to her apartment to pack a bag. And she'd let her hair down. Literally.

Her blond hair hung down in a silky sheet just past her shoulders. His fingers itched to touch the strands. Had he always had this fascination with hair? Or was it just hers?

She wore a kelly green turtleneck beneath a black leather jacket and jeans tucked into calf-high black boots with low heels. Her gold shield and sidearm were at her waist, as a reminder that she was working and not on vacation.

"You'll have to come back when you can," he stated softly. "The Smithsonian museums are world-class."

Excitement lit up her eyes. "You remember them?"

He gave her a wry grin. "Not really. It's more of a vague recollection than an actual memory. I don't know if what I see in my mind is from experience or pictures. But I feel certain that you'd like the various aspects of the museums."

"I'm sure I would. I'm especially interested in the American first ladies collection."

He grinned. "Do you have aspirations of being a first lady?"

She returned his grin. "No, if I wanted to live in the White House it would be as president."

He chuckled at her declaration. He admired her pluck

and confidence. It would take a special man to contend with this woman.

"I like seeing strong women prevail," she continued. "And you have to admit, it would take a certain amount of courage to be married to the president of the United States."

"True." What kind of courage would it take to marry a man with no memory?

Wow, that was a leap. He wasn't even sure how he felt about this pretty, capable and determined deputy. Letting his mind and heart venture down the perilous road of romance wasn't smart. The last thing he wanted was to hurt Audrey or anyone else.

Did he have someone waiting for his return? Not a wife, he knew, but a girlfriend? Where did he even reside? Canada was a big place.

His gaze strayed to the man at the wheel. Blake Fallon would have the answers Nathanial sought.

But did he want to ask? Would the answers bring pain or trigger his memories?

Didn't he owe it to Audrey, for saving his sorry hide, and to himself to dig into his past and uncover who he was?

Fear that he'd not like the answers bubbled inside him, adding to his headache. When he could get Blake alone, he'd seek the answers despite his trepidations. Better to hear who he was without worrying about Audrey's reaction. He hated the thought of her thinking less of him. He leaned back against the headrest and closed his eyes against the pain throbbing in his head. Soon enough he'd find the courage to confront his past.

The vehicle rolled to a stop in the underground garage of a nondescript building, and they were hustled inside to a conference room on a high floor with a direct view of the Washington Monument. Nathanial went to the window.

Was this why the monolith seemed so familiar? Had he stood in this room before, this exact spot, even?

"It's beautiful," Audrey commented as she halted at his side.

He turned to look at her. She was beautiful. And sweet and had a core of steel that he respected and admired. "Yes. Very beautiful."

She slanted him a quick glance as if she somehow suspected he wasn't referring to the tall stone pillar.

"Welcome back from the dead, Officer Longhorn," a deep voice intoned from behind them.

Nathanial and Audrey turned toward the room. Nathanial's gaze landed on the man standing at the head of the conference table. He was tall and distinguished looking in a well-tailored dark suit, white button-down shirt and burgundy tie. His salt-and-pepper hair was swept back from his angular face and sharp deep blue eyes assessed them. Nathanial assumed this must be Director Moore of Homeland Security.

"And welcome, Deputy Martin," Moore continued as he skirted around the table toward Audrey. "We owe you a huge thank-you."

She met him with her hand outstretched. "Not a problem, sir." They shook hands. "Doing my job."

"And doing it well, from what I've heard," he replied. Then he shifted his focus to Nathanial. "You look well, but I understand you have no memory of your work with IBETs."

"No, sir, I don't," Nathanial replied, accepting the man's offer of a handshake. He had a strong and firm grip but didn't squeeze his hand in a show of power, which Nathanial appreciated. "I hope you'll forgive me my ignorance. IBETs?"

"Integrated Border Enforcement Taskforce, a joint effort

by the Canadians and the United States to keep our mutual boundary line secure." Moore gestured to the chairs. "Have a seat, Nathanial, Deputy."

Nathanial pulled out a chair for Audrey. She arched an eyebrow, and her mouth curved into a slight smile, but she made no comment as she took her seat. He claimed the chair next to her, bumping his knees against hers. Awareness of how close she was raced over him, making him ruefully shake his head. What was he, a junior higher with his first crush?

No, but he was a man without a memory, crushing on the woman who'd saved his life. *Better snap out of it*, he told himself. He really needed to have a discussion with Blake. He forced his attention to the director.

"We'd like you to meet with our doctors here," the director was saying as he leaned a hip against the table. "Not that we don't trust Dr. Martin's assessment, but we do have the most advanced therapies and practices in the country, if not the world, at our disposal."

"Yes, sir." Nathanial didn't have a problem meeting with anyone who could potentially help him regain his faculties. He shushed the nervous voice inside his head that questioned if he really wanted to know. Instead, he sent up a silent prayer that he'd be strong enough to withstand whatever he discovered.

"Deputy Martin, I'll have someone escort you to your hotel while Officer Longhorn meets with the docs."

"With all due respect, sir, where Nathanial goes, I go," Audrey said in a tone that was courteous but firm, leaving no doubt her words weren't a request but a fact.

The director matched her level gaze with one of his own. Nathanial waited to see if the director would try to match her resolve, but then the man smiled and he spared Nathanial an amused look.

"Well, it seems you have your very own bodyguard, Nathanial." Moore straightened. "I have an escort ready to take you and your guest to Walter Reed medical center."

"Thank you, Director Moore," Audrey said and rose from her chair.

Nathanial stood and shook the man's hand again. For some reason Director Moore inspired a sense of trust.

"If you'll follow me." Moore moved to the conference room door.

Audrey hesitated, obviously waiting for Nathanial to take a step, but his gaze once again went to the lone obelisk standing like a sentry over the city, the white lights highlighting the gray stone. A sense of loneliness swamped Nathanial. A forgotten memory surfaced, sharp and desolate. Him as a child of maybe seven, standing in front of a Christmas tree only half-decorated, while voices shouted and shrieked from another room. Fear and anger roiled in his gut, his small fists clenched at his sides. Who did the voices belong to? Why was he so upset?

Nathanial tried to hold on to the recollection, to expand it, to make the memory clear, but it slipped away, leaving him feeling strangely hollow.

"Nathanial?"

Audrey's voice brought him back to the present. Aware of the director's gaze, he kept the snippet of recall to himself. "Sorry, I was distracted by the view."

He followed the director out of the room with Audrey's hand gently folded in his.

Audrey paced outside the closed office door of one of the country's top psychiatrists. Or so she and Nathanial had been informed. Nathanial had stepped inside the office over an hour ago and hadn't emerged. Audrey was growing antsy.

The ding of the elevator brought her gaze from the waxed linoleum floor in time to see Blake Fallon step out of the car. His handsome features were dark with worry as he strode toward her, stopping a couple feet away as if afraid to get too close. But why? What made the man wary of her?

"Is he still in with Dr. Pembley?" Blake asked, his voice deep and cutting.

Audrey straightened her shoulders, unwilling to let this man's sheer size and commanding presence intimidate her. "Yes."

"So what's the story?" Blake asked, his gaze narrowing. "What is it you want from Nathanial?"

Audrey tilted her head. "Want?"

"I've never seen him so dependent, especially on a woman," he said.

Interesting. Not sure how to address the complicated levels that tidbit opened up, she went for the obvious and honest answer. "He's in a vulnerable state right now. I'm only here to discover the truth and to protect him."

"I can do that."

"He isn't ready to trust you."

Hurt flashed across Blake's face. "He was—is my best friend. He's a good guy. Someone I trusted my life with, someone I trusted to have my back."

"But now you're not so sure."

A frown marred Blake's brow. "I am sure. The man I know wouldn't have willingly put his team in danger. Something bad happened." His fingers curled into fists. "He needs to remember."

Empathy unfurled inside her chest. "He will. And he'll be that man again. He just needs some time." She sent up a quick prayer that Nathanial's memories would return sooner rather than later. Or worse yet, not at all. "Tell me about him. About who he was before I found him on the beach."

Blake raked a hand through his dark hair, making the already tousled strands even more unruly. A gold wedding band on his ring finger glinted beneath the overhead lights. "We would joke that Nathanial was *ka peyakot mahihkan*— a lone wolf."

Surprise washed over her. "You speak Cree?"

"Just a few words that Nathanial taught me."

She digested the statement. *Lone wolf.* "What do you mean by *lone wolf*? He doesn't play well with others?"

One corner of Blake's mouth lifted. "He does. It's not that. He prefers recon missions and to be on watch."

She remembered he'd said that had been Nathanial's job on the assignment. "And in his personal life?" She hated the heat creeping up her neck, but she was curious. For his sake, not hers. *Right. And pigs fly.*

Wariness flared in Blake's eyes. "He's unattached, if that's what you're wondering."

She shrugged. "Just asking."

"The last thing he needs right now is his heart being tethered to you," Blake said with warning in his tone.

Though she appreciated Blake watching out for his friend, she didn't need the counsel. She wasn't looking to tether her heart to anyone, least of all Nathanial. She might like him, care for him, even, but that was a long way from tethering. From loving.

The door to the office opened. Audrey's heart leaped as Nathanial walked out and reached for her hand.

"I remembered something."

TEN

"That's good, right?" Audrey gripped his hands.

A rush of warmth traveled up Nathanial's arms at the contact. He should have told her about the memory back at the IBETs headquarters, but the sudden flood of images and sensations he'd experienced had made him feel too raw, too vulnerable. Still did. But it was a step in the right direction toward regaining his past.

Blake lurched forward. "You remember what happened to you on that rooftop?" Blake's urgent, hopeful tone twisted bitter regret within Nathanial.

Nathanial flicked a glance at the agent. "No, unfortunately."

Blake blew out a frustrated breath. Nathanial didn't blame Blake for his frustration. Men had died, and the key to bringing those men's killers to justice lay locked within Nathanial's skull. If only they could hook him up to some sort of machine that could pull out the memories.

Nathanial focused on Audrey. "I remembered something from my childhood. An image of a Christmas tree."

He didn't know what had triggered the memory, but Dr. Pembley had been able to draw out more of the details of the tree, with dangling homemade ornaments and the house filled with the scents of wood smoke and gingerbread. They agreed this was probably his childhood home. As for the yelling voices, the doctor speculated it could be from that time or another memory that was trying to come through. Hopefully the memory of what had happened to him on that rooftop. "The doc suggests I travel to my childhood home, since that seems to be where my mind wants to go."

Audrey tilted her head. "In Saskatchewan?"

He shrugged and turned his attention on Blake. "You said that is where I'm from. Do you have an address for my family?" His heart bumped. Were his parents still alive? Did he have brothers or sisters? A wife? He slipped his hands from Audrey's and stuffed them into the pockets of his jacket. Why couldn't he keep a distance from this woman?

"I do. I'll take you there," Blake offered.

Anxiety knotted his chest. He didn't want to go with Blake, even though it would be the wisest decision. A decision he had to make, because he needed to release Audrey. Though from the way her lush lips pressed together, he had a feeling she wouldn't cooperate. She'd made it clear that she would see this, whatever this was, through to the end.

"I appreciate the offer," Nathanial finally said. "No offense intended, but Audrey and I can make it there on our own."

"Not happening." Blake stepped closer. There was no mistaking the hurt beneath the man's hard exterior. "If you don't want me to accompany you, fine. But you need a team with you. I'm sure the Kelleys wouldn't mind the trip and would provide more protection."

"The Kelleys?" Nathanial felt as if he should know who they were, but the knowledge was just out of his mind's reach.

Blake huffed out a breath rife with exasperation. "Drew and his wife, Sami."

"The Mountie?" Audrey asked.

Barely sparing her a glance, Blake nodded. "Yes. His wife is FBI and works for the US legal attaché to Canada. They would make the perfect escort for you both."

Nathanial sensed an undercurrent of strain between Blake and Audrey. He wondered what had happened between them while he was in with the doctor. He looked to Audrey to see what she thought of the backup plan.

She shrugged. "Couldn't hurt to have more protection."

He nodded. "All right, then."

Having the couple along would provide a barrier between him and Audrey, too. He needed a buffer, something to keep him from giving in to the temptation to kiss the pretty sheriff's deputy. Because the need to do so hovered close to the surface any time she was near. He inwardly sighed as he followed the others to the parking garage. He had to get a grip.

Blake drove Nathanial and Audrey to a popular hotel chain a few blocks away from the IBETs headquarters. The lobby was quiet as they waited near a warm gas fireplace while Blake checked them in at the registration desk. Overhead, chandeliers gleamed with multiple lights. Marble floors covered with intricately woven area rugs provided texture and comfy seating invited lingering. A thirty-foot Douglas fir tree adorned in gold ornaments and shiny gold ribbon took center stage in the lobby.

Nathanial's curiosity prompted him to ask Audrey as he sat on a dark cherry-colored chair. "What's going on between you and Blake?"

As she took the seat across from him, she seemed to consider her words before speaking. "Nothing, really. He's concerned about you and wants to make sure you don't end up hurt."

Something in her tone made him think she and Blake weren't only referring to his physical well-being. Had Blake warned her off for some reason? Pain lanced through his head. He winced.

Audrey leaned forward to touch his knee. "You okay?"

The concern in her voice touched him. She cared. The knowledge filled him with pleasure that he quickly tamped down. So much for getting a grip. Her care and concern were born of her job, not from any heartfelt affection. They barely knew each other. The irony that he knew more about her than he did about himself nearly made him laugh, but the mirth died a fast death as helpless anger clawed through him. He wanted his memories, his life, back. Whoever had robbed him of both would pay a high price.

Blake's approach drew Nathanial's attention. There was something familiar about the man that seemed to knock at Nathanial's consciousness. Knowledge of their shared past taunted him, just out of reach, ratcheting up his frustration several notches.

"Your rooms are next to each other," the ICE agent said as he handed over the key cards.

Taking the card holder from him, Nathanial decided he needed answers. "Audrey, you go on up. I would like a moment with Blake." He held up his hand as storm clouds gathered in her eyes. "Please."

Her gaze bounced between him and Blake before she said to Blake, "You'll see that he gets safely to his room?"

"Of course." Blake's affronted tone made her scowl.

Though Nathanial appreciated their concern, he didn't like being talked about as if he were a child. "I can get myself to the room, thank you very much."

A smile slid across Audrey's face. "I didn't mean to imply you couldn't."

He narrowed his gaze at her placating tone, but instead of offending him, her words touched him. "You're worried about me. I get it. But apparently I can handle myself."

The concern didn't leave her gaze. "But you don't have a weapon with you."

Her statement stirred hesitation within him. Could he handle himself in a hand-to-hand situation? Was using a sniper rifle or a knife the only means he had to defend himself? Doubts swirled. But his need for answers outweighed his need for self-preservation. "Go on. I'll be up shortly, and I'll even knock on your door to let you know I arrived in one piece."

Though it was clear from the worry in her pretty eyes that she didn't like leaving him, she inclined her head and walked to the elevator. As soon as she stepped inside and the doors closed, Nathanial spoke to Blake. "What did you say to Audrey? She seemed upset."

Blake snorted. "I told her what I'm going to tell you. Don't go getting all goofy over the deputy. She's not your type."

"I have a type?" Nathanial would have thought leggy blondes with attitude would be right up his alley. At least this particular one was.

"Yes, you do. Ones that aren't looking for forever," Blake stated and moved to sit on one end of the couch in the lobby.

The heat from the gas fireplace buffeted Nathanial as he followed Blake, sat in the chair and leaned in so his voice wouldn't carry despite the fact they were alone in the lounge area. "So I don't have any *one* special lady pining away for me?" He needed to confirm what Blake was saying. Not having a girlfriend waiting for him was good news and eased some of the guilt at his attraction to Audrey constricting his chest. He still wasn't sure he was good enough for the pretty deputy.

"Oh, I'm sure there are women across both borders who'd be more than willing to be your special someone," Blake replied dryly. "But no." He let out a wry chuckle. "You date. A lot. But you don't get serious."

That didn't sound so good. "Why not?"

Blake shrugged. "How should I know? You always boast you like your freedom. I don't want to see you making a decision that affects your future out of some misguided sense of gratitude for Audrey saving your life."

Digesting that statement left a cold spot in Nathanial's heart. He was a serial dater? Afraid of commitment? But why? What had happened in his past to make him want to be free of relationships?

Blake's lips twisted in ironic amusement. "But you were more than happy to push me toward my wife, Liz. Let's see, you told me I was afraid of feeling." He let out a chuckle. "You were right, as you usually are. I was afraid."

Hearing the other man talk about something Nathanial had said in the past sent a fresh sliver of pain slicing through Nathanial's brain. He wanted to remember the conversation. To remember what it had been like to see this man fall in love. Nathanial assumed Liz was now Blake's wife. "You married her."

"I did. Best decision I ever made." Love for his bride shone in his dark eyes. "We live on Hilton Head Island." His happiness dimmed. "You've been to the house several times."

Nathanial's chest caved slightly. "You said I was your best man at your wedding. So I take it you and I know—knew—each other well."

Blake splayed his hands on his knees. "Yes." He reached

inside the breast pocket of his overcoat for his wallet. He flipped it open to reveal two photographs. One of his bride, an attractive honey blonde that Nathanial didn't recognize.

The other image was a group shot of at least eight men dressed in tuxedos. Nathanial recognized the members of the IBETs team he'd recently reconnected with. Nathanial had his arm slung around Blake's shoulders while mugging for the camera. Staring at the photo, Nathanial fought his faulty mind, desperate to recall this day when he'd appeared to be happy. A splitting headache was his compensation.

Rubbing at his temple, he said, "Tell me about the mission."

Blake put the wallet away. "We'd been tracking the movements of Sergei Kosloff, a Russian immigrant to the US. Over the past few years he's been slowly building his empire, dealing in arms, drugs, human trafficking…you name it.

"An informant within his organization flipped for a reduced sentence. Naming dates and times of illegal weapons crossing the US–Canada border. Our task was to seize this latest shipment and turn as many of his men as we could in hopes of finding Kosloff's base of operation.

"We know it's somewhere on the East Coast and that he has connections in several states where firearms are bought, then transported to other states before they're finally smuggled into Canada. From there many of the weapons are dispersed within Canada, but some are also transported to Europe."

Nathanial scrubbed a hand over his jaw. "The man we captured at the Calico Bay sheriff's department had had an Eastern European accent."

"That's what Sheriff Crump said. He, no doubt, worked

for Kosloff but he didn't come up in any database. He must have been new to the organization."

"And Kosloff had him killed," Nathanial pointed out. Clearly the master criminal didn't like loose ends. Was Nathanial one of Kosloff's loose ends? Had he been working for Kosloff as Chase suggested? The thought tied his insides into knots. "Have you checked all the team members for any unexplainable payouts?" He held his breath, waiting for the answer and hoping nothing showed in his own bank account.

"I did. Came up empty."

A small measure of relief filled Nathanial. But they were no closer to solving the mystery of who and why. He hated to think he'd been involved with Kosloff. But the possibility lingered like a bad odor.

Going home might be the only way to regain his memory, the only way to clear his own name and find the guilty party.

Anxiety kicked up in his gut. A part of him was afraid to remember, but he had to know—good guy or bad?

Audrey freshened up in her hotel room. The view from the bedroom window overlooked the Capitol Building. The sun had set while she waited for Nathanial to reach his room. The world had been cast into inky shadows broken by the glow of a million lights—streetlamps, inside the many buildings and monuments, and the cars crawling along the avenues.

Despite the cheer of Christmas decorations everywhere, there was franticness about the city that made her antsy. Or it could be she was worried that something would happen to Nathanial and she wouldn't be there to protect him.

The slight knock on the door connecting her room to

the next had her heart jumping. She hurried to the door and yanked it open.

Backlit by the glow of the lamp on the dresser, Nathanial grinned. "Miss me?"

She had, but she wasn't going to admit it. "Glad to see you made it alive."

She brushed past him to enter his room, which was laid out exactly like her own. A new suitcase sat on the bed, the tag still hanging from the handle. Inside the bag were some fresh clothes.

"I stopped in the gift shop before coming up."

"Good idea." Though she didn't like the idea of him wandering around unprotected. She went to the window and studied the line of sight from the buildings across the street. Not detecting anything untoward, she closed the room-darkening curtains. "Stay away from the window. If anyone knocks on your door, don't answer. Come knock on my door."

He didn't acknowledge her comment, but instead asked, "Are you hungry?"

She hadn't thought about food. But she knew they both needed to eat to keep up their energy. "I'll order room service."

"We could head downstairs to the restaurant."

"Better to stay out of sight," she said. "We don't know if your pursuers have found out where we are. We need to keep an extra-low profile so we can make it safely to your home."

Seeming to accept her pronouncement, he picked up the room service menu. "Then we'll dine in. I think the blue cheese hamburger, fries and a side garden salad sound good." He handed her the menu.

"I'll take care of it." She headed toward the connecting door, but he stepped into her path.

"I don't think I'm the kind of man who lets others take care of him."

She arched an eyebrow as her heart rate ticked upward. "You know this how?"

His wide shoulders lifted and fell. "Just a feeling. I get all twitchy when you get bossy and mothering." He softened his teasing words with a smile.

She pressed her lips together to keep from grimacing. She'd heard similar statements before. The jerk from college, Kyle, had claimed that was one of the reasons he'd cheated on her—he couldn't take her controlling nature. She couldn't help it if taking charge came naturally. Not only did her job require her to be in command of every situation, but she also came by her bossiness honestly. Her mother had the same trait, which made her good at her job of running the Calico Bay Medical Center.

Nathanial narrowed his gaze. "I've upset you. I'm sorry."

She shoved her shoulders back and lifted her chin. "I'm doing my job, Nathanial. Putting your safety first is my priority." She stepped around him, needing to put some space between them. She didn't want him digging into her psyche. It was bad enough she'd told him about Kyle—she didn't want to humiliate herself further with the details. "I'll make the order."

"You do that."

His amused toned chased her back to her room. She put in the order for two hamburgers, fries and side salads, and a pot of coffee. She would need to stay alert in case the men trying to kill Nathanial took the opportunity of striking in the middle of the night.

Fifteen minutes later there was a knock on her hotel door. With a hand on her weapon, she checked the peephole. A man dressed in the hotel's green, black and gold livery stood on the other side of the door with a cart bearing two silver domes presumably covering their dinner.

She signed for the food and wheeled the cart in, tipped the man and sent him on his way. A second later another knock sounded at the door. Nathanial. She opened the door and stepped back.

Nathanial poked his head inside the room. "Dinner?" He entered, closing the door behind him.

"Yes." She lifted the lids, and the most delicious smells wafted up, making her stomach cramp with hunger.

They each took a plate and sat. Nathanial took the desk chair while she took the cushy chair in the corner.

For a moment both were content to eat in silence.

"Blake told me about the mission I was on," Nathanial said as he set his half-eaten burger back on the plate.

She listened, riveted, as he spoke about the criminal Kosloff. She wiped her hands on a napkin. "Did Blake say whether he'd checked the team's financials?"

"I asked and he had. Nothing to report there."

Reaching for her tablet, she did a quick search in the national criminal database for Sergei Kosloff and found a photo. She held it up for Nathanial to view. Sergei Kosloff had a round face, with wide-set eyes and dark hair. "Now we not only have a name but a face for the man who's trying to kill you."

She watched Nathanial closely for any flare of recognition, but none came as he studied the image.

His mouth twisted. "But the question is, why does he want me dead? What threat do I pose?"

Questions she prayed would be answered soon.

The next morning Nathanial and Audrey stood in the lobby of the hotel waiting to meet their escort to Saskatchewan. Nathanial couldn't take his eyes off Audrey. He was struck once again by her beauty. Not just the outward package. Though that was certainly pleasing. She wore loose wool trousers and a lightweight sweater and had a coat folded over her arm. Her blond hair was loose again, falling about her shoulder with one side tucked behind her ear.

He also found her intellect and determination appealing. Her alert gaze swept the lobby and the street outside the window. To the world she most likely appeared at ease, with her legs braced slightly apart and her right foot marginally forward in a stance that looked natural but also afforded her an anchor and a push-off point.

She was nervous. Her fingers drummed on her hipbone, much like he'd seen her do on her utility belt when she was in uniform.

Blake had called them first thing in the morning saying they were booked on an 8 a.m. flight to Saskatoon with a short layover in Minneapolis, and from there they would drive three hours to Nathanial's hometown of Pierceland. Anticipation revved in his veins. Remembering was paramount to solving this case and to taking back control of his life.

The knowledge had promptly given him a rip-roaring headache.

A black Suburban pulled to the curb outside the hotel door. Blake climbed from behind the wheel while Luke Wellborn jumped out of the passenger seat.

"Here's our ride," Nathanial said to Audrey. He grabbed her bag and the small one he'd purchased for himself in the hotel's gift shop. Grateful that she didn't put up a fuss, they headed outside. The frosty air bit at him. He pulled the corners of the wool-and-shearling coat closer, thankful Deputy Paulson had let him borrow it.

Luke took the bags and stowed them in the far back while Blake opened the back passenger door for them to slide onto the bench seat. Once everyone was secured inside the vehicle, Blake took off, expertly weaving through the early-morning traffic.

"Drew and Sami will meet you at the airport in Saskatoon," Blake informed them.

Snow began falling, gently coating the world in a blanket of white, reminding Nathanial Christmas was only days away. He sent up a silent prayer that he'd have his memory, his life, back by then.

When they landed in Saskatoon, they were met by Drew Kelley and his wife, Sami Bennett-Kelley. Both were dressed in what Nathanial would call work attire—Drew wore black slacks, jackboots and a warm-looking midlength wool peacoat. There was the slight bulge at his side where he no doubt carried a firearm.

Nathanial nodded a greeting to Drew before studying Sami. She was petite, with a wild head of curls and alert blue eyes, and was also dressed in dark slacks and a red button-down top beneath a short, thick leather jacket. She yanked a black glove off her right hand and thrust her hand out to Audrey.

"Deputy Martin," Sami said in a clipped voice. "Thank you for all you're doing for this one." She tipped her chin in Nathanial's direction.

"You're welcome." Audrey matched the FBI agent's formal tone.

Sami turned her vivid gaze to him, and there was no mistaking the affection in her eyes. "No memory, huh?"

He grimaced and shook his head, already liking the direct way the woman took on life. "Sorry."

She shrugged. "Unless you've gone dirty, no apology needed." She reached out and took his hand. Her fingers were strong as they curled over his. "We're glad you're alive. We were worried you weren't."

Nathanial accepted her welcome and her concern. These people had cared about him. And still did. Warmth spread through his chest, taking the edge off his headache.

They hustled from the smaller airport to an American-made super-duty dual-cab truck marked with the RCMP initials and logo.

Sami climbed in front with Drew taking the wheel while Audrey and Nathanial took the back passenger seats. Sami kept up a running dialogue, asking questions and commenting on the passing scenery. Seemed this was her first time in this part of Canada.

Nathanial had hoped seeing the landscape of his birthplace would jog something loose inside his brain, but the flat, snowy countryside was unfamiliar. Groves of trees dusted with white powder dotted large stretches of undeveloped pastures.

"Hey, look." Sami's excited tone made Nathanial smile. "What is that?"

A large, dark-colored animal stood off in the distance. Its compact body was covered with thick fur, and the beast's snout was long and rounded at the end. Flat antlers rose off its head.

Môswa. The word floated through Nathanial's brain. Was this more of the Cree language that apparently he'd been speaking when he first awoke in the hospital? Was the word the name for the creature in the pasture?

"Prairie moose," Drew said with a grin. "Sami grew up in the Pacific Northwest."

Moose. Nathanial was pretty sure he'd just named the animal in Cree.

"They don't have moose on the West Coast?" Audrey asked.

"Oh, they do somewhere, I'm sure," Sami explained.

"But I grew up on the coast of Oregon then moved to Portland. I've never seen anything that big."

"What's this?" Drew asked, drawing Nathanial's focus
to a car pulled to the side of the road about fifty yards
ahead.

Drew took his foot off the gas.

"Probably someone stopping to take a picture of the
moose," Sami said, but there was a thread of tension in
her tone.

"Or someone with car trouble," Audrey ventured, but
she didn't sound convinced. She put her hand on his shoulder. "Slide down, just in case."

Nathanial wanted to argue. No way could anyone be
gunning for him out here. Could they?

As the gap between the truck and the car closed, all the
doors on the sedan popped open. Four gunmen jumped out
and aimed semiautomatic weapons at the truck.

ELEVEN

As bullets riddled the heavy-duty truck and shattered the back window, raining pebbles of safety glass onto them, Audrey's heart slammed against her rib cage, and she screamed, "Get down!"

She yanked Nathanial's arm at the exact moment he pushed her to the truck's back passenger floorboard, toppling onto her. His weight forced the air from her lungs.

"Hang on!" Drew shouted. The truck engine roared, tires dug into the layer of snow and the vehicle fishtailed before finding traction and shooting forward, passing the car and the men. A barrage of gunfire hit the truck, the pinging of bullets echoing in Audrey's head as she did her best to protect Nathanial. But he wasn't cooperating. He kept trying to shield her.

"Hey! I'm supposed to be protecting you," she grumbled, her voice muffled into his chest. The scent of the hotel soap mingled with his masculine scent, and if she weren't so mad and admittedly scared, she'd have snuggled closer.

He braced his elbows on either side of her head to keep from crushing her. "You can be the bullet stopper next time," he muttered huskily, close to her ear.

Their faces were close, so close she could see herself

reflected in his dark eyes. His promise of a kiss screamed through her mind, and she had the wildest urge to lift her head off the floor and press her lips to his.

Frustration whipped at her back, and embarrassment heated her skin. She would not give in to her attraction to this man, despite the affection embedding itself in her heart. She pushed at him as best she could, since her arms were trapped. He might not remember being a law officer, but his reflexes were in working order. The instinct to duck and cover and protect was strong in him, strong enough that he'd overpowered her by sheer muscle strength.

The truck continued to career down the road. The onslaught of bullets lessened until the only noises were the tires against the snowy road, the icy wind whistling through the cab and Sami calling in the attack, her voice clipped and concise. Nathanial dropped his forehead next to Audrey's, and he relaxed as if his body had deflated. Pressure built in Audrey's chest. Her breath lay entombed in her lungs. Panic clawed at her. Had he been hit?

"Nathanial?" Audrey's heart faltered. "Nathanial? Are you okay?" She couldn't keep alarm from creeping into her tone.

He stirred and eased off her, allowing her to breathe. He blinked and shook his head. "I blacked out for a second." His dark eyes searched her face. "Are you hurt?"

Her relief that he was not injured was immediately chased away by her need to take back control of the situation. "No, I'm not hurt, but you will be if you don't get off me," she ground out between clenched teeth.

The corner of his mouth lifted in challenge. He had her pinned to the truck floor. There was no way to bring her knee up or room for her hands to reach her weapon. He glanced up toward the top of the bench seat, where Drew and Sami sat. "Is it safe?"

"Yes" came Drew's terse reply.

The truck hadn't slowed down. Were they being chased? "You heard the man—it's safe. Get. Off. Me."

"Right." He crawled onto the backseat, but kept his head down. He brushed glass off his shoulders and off the seat for her.

She sat up and stifled a groan at the aches and pains shooting through her back and hips. She accepted his offered hand of help and scooted onto the seat. The road stretched out in front of them as the truck barreled onward. Audrey glanced out the busted-out back window. The car full of armed men chased after them. The little sedan didn't have the weight or the studded tires of the truck and began to fall back. Audrey sent up a quick prayer that the gunmen didn't have more men waiting up ahead to box them in.

The sound of sirens drew closer. Up ahead three identical small SUVs with flashing lights and the RCMP logo rushed toward them. Audrey whipped her attention behind them and watched the sedan slow, whip a U-turn and race away in the opposite direction. Drew brought the truck to a halt. One of the SUVs halted beside them while the other two zipped past in hot pursuit of the armed men in the sedan.

Drew rolled down his window, and the driver of the SUV did the same.

"Inspector Cavendish," the man introduced himself.

"Inspector Kelley," Drew replied and quickly explained the situation.

"I'll let my men know to be careful," Cavendish assured him. "Follow me to the station. We'll need statements."

Drew waited for the other Mountie to turn his vehicle around, then they followed him for several minutes on the lonely stretch of road cutting through the prairie until they came to civilization. They rolled through the small

town of Meadow Lake. The low-roofed buildings lining
the main street held a certain charm that made Audrey
think of Calico Bay, though here the terrain was flat and
trees in planters provided a little greenery.

Audrey noticed Nathanial's clenched jaw and his hands
gripping his thighs.

"You okay?"

He met her gaze. She sucked in a breath at the torment
in his dark eyes.

"I don't know."

"You said you blacked out." She covered one of his
hands with her own. "What happened?"

"I had a flash of memory." He turned his hand over
and laced his fingers with hers. For a moment the sight of
their entwined hands distracted her. "I think it was from
the rooftop."

Her gaze jerked up to meet his. "Tell me."

He closed his eyes. "I was lying on the roof, looking
through the scope on my rifle." His brow furrowed. "A
noise." With his free hand, he rubbed at his temple. "I
rolled to my back." He shook his head with a grimace.
"That's it." He opened his eyes. "Something hovers right
at the edge of my mind, but every time I try to hang on to
it…" He gave a shrug.

She squeezed his hand. "You'll remember."

He looked away, as if not ready to acknowledge her en-
couragement. "We're here."

The vehicle halted outside a one-story brick building.
The Canadian flag flew from a twelve-foot flagpole next
to the sidewalk near the front door, and a blue sign with
the RCMP logo was planted in the middle of what Audrey
guessed would be a lawn in the warmer seasons but now
was covered in snow. Drew turned off the engine. "We
have to assume we're being tracked."

"We found one tracker in Nathanial's boot, but he tossed it out the window a long time ago," Audrey stated.

"Doesn't mean there couldn't be more tracking devices. We all need to check our clothing," Drew stated grimly. "I'll check the vehicle as well."

They piled out of the truck. The temperature outside had dropped below zero. Shivering from the onslaught of frigid air, Audrey made quick work of checking her clothing and found nothing then shoved her hands into her coat pockets.

"Found it!" Drew held up a small wireless GPS tracker. "It was tucked inside my to-go bag." He threw it on the ground and smashed it with his heel.

The unspoken concern that someone close to them had planted the device had them all on edge.

They followed Inspector Cavendish inside, where they gave him their statements. By the time they were done, the two Mounties who'd given pursuit of the gunmen returned empty-handed.

One of the men, a big burly guy with shorn blond hair and green eyes, stopped and stared at Nathanial. "Hey, I know you."

Beside her, Nathanial tensed. "Do you?"

"Yes. You grew up near here, eh?"

"Apparently so." Nathanial held out his hand. "Nathanial Longhorn."

"Kurt Siebol." The man grasped Nathanial's hand. "You played point guard for Pierceland Center High. I remember playing against you my senior year. You were good."

"Thanks." Nathanial turned to Audrey. "I played basketball."

She smiled at the wonder in his voice. She'd have liked to have seen him on the court. She was sure he'd have moved with the same easy agility he displayed as an adult.

Inspector Cavendish offered them the use of one of

their official vehicles. After saying goodbye, they headed to Pierceland with Kurt providing an escort. Once they hit the town, Kurt waved farewell and headed back to Meadow Lake.

They stopped at a small hotel and secured rooms before venturing to the heart of the town. To say Pierceland was small was an understatement. Stand-alone buildings dotted the snow-covered main drive. A gas station, credit union and village post office lined one side of the road. Across the street stood a grocery store and a restaurant called Bartlett's Family Dining.

"Stop here," Nathanial said. "Let's go into the restaurant."

Audrey eyed the welcome sign in the front window—Family Owned and Operated for Fifty Years.

"Do you recognize this place?" Sami asked before Audrey could.

"I don't know. It seems familiar," Nathanial said. "I want to stop."

Drew and Sami exchanged concerned looks. "We still need to be careful."

"I'll only be a moment." Nathanial leaned forward. "Pull in around the back, out of sight."

Drew circled the building and brought the borrowed Mountie vehicle to a halt near the back door.

"I'm going in," Nathanial said with a determination that let them all know there was no way they'd be able to stop him unless they knocked him out.

Audrey hurried to his side. She'd at least do her best to keep him safe.

"Make it quick," Drew instructed Nathanial as they rounded the building for the entrance. He and Sami took up positions where they had a clear view of the road out front.

Audrey was thankful for the restaurant's warmth seeping into her bones. A string of bells attached to the door jingled when the door shut behind them.

The restaurant wasn't crowded; only a few tables were occupied. And those that were there turned to stare at the newcomers. Cheery Christmas decorations hung from the rafters. A line of stocking cutouts danced across the front desk, where a woman stood behind the counter. She wore an oxford cotton shirt with the restaurant's logo on the right breast pocket. Her dark hair hung in a tight braid over her left shoulder.

"Good afternoon," the woman said with a smile. Then her gaze landed on Nathanial, and she paled and her smile fell away. "What are you doing here?"

Audrey stepped next to Nathanial as a strange sensation of protectiveness and possessiveness surged through her. Drew and Sami took positions behind them as if ready to jump in.

He cocked his head and stared at the woman. "I'm sorry," he said. "I don't remember your name."

The woman took a step back as if shock gave way to anger. "Really? You're going with that?" Her gaze flicked to Audrey and then back to Nathanial. "Is this your wife?"

"No, this—" His words cut off as he slanted Audrey a glance.

Clearly he was at a loss how to explain what he was going through. Audrey decided to borrow a page from her great-uncle's playbook—*when in doubt, stick to the facts.* She flashed the badge fastened to her belt at her waist. "Deputy Audrey Martin with the Calico Bay, Maine, sheriff's department. Officer Longhorn suffered a blow to the head and is suffering retrograde amnesia. We're hopeful he'll regain his memories here where he grew up."

The woman's brown eyes widened. Her rose-colored

lips formed an O. "I didn't think things like that really happened."

"They do," Nathanial said softly. "I take it we knew each other."

Confusion stole over face. "Yes. I'm Laurie. Laurie Bartlett. You really don't remember me?"

What was the story between Nathanial and Laurie? "We're you two close?" Audrey asked Laurie.

Laurie's mouth twisted in a half grimace. "High school. We were high school sweethearts."

Over a decade ago. And yet Audrey had the feeling Laurie still carried a torch for Nathanial. The knowledge burned in Audrey's chest. She didn't like the jealousy stirring to life. She had no claim on Nathanial.

Whatever the outcome and wherever this journey took him, Audrey would be returning to her own life in Calico Bay. Alone. Becoming upset over Nathanial's old flame was wrong on so many levels.

She needed to shore up the walls around her heart and keep perspective. Even though she liked Nathanial and was attracted to him, she had to find a way to keep an emotional distance.

"Your family owns this restaurant," Nathanial stated. "That's why it seemed familiar."

Laurie nodded. "Yes. You used to work here. We worked here together."

"Can you tell me how to get to my parents' home?"

"Sure. I can do that." Laurie grabbed a piece of paper and scribbled down the directions. "They'll be glad to see you."

Taking the piece of paper she offered, Nathanial said, "Thank you, Laurie. I appreciate your help." He hesitated. "And I'm sorry I don't remember you."

Laurie shrugged and walked away, leaving them standing in the entryway.

Audrey didn't buy Laurie's nonchalance. She was upset and trying hard not to let it show.

"That was interesting," Sami said beneath her breath. "I guess we're not eating here."

"We've worn out our welcome," Drew's deep voice intoned.

They left the restaurant. Audrey glanced back to see Laurie watching them through the window. She climbed into the truck next to Nathanial. He handed Drew the directions.

On the drive along the country road leading to his family home, Nathanial leaned forward to ask Drew, "Did you know about Laurie? Had I ever mentioned her?"

Audrey's pulse ticked up. She watched Drew meet Nathanial's gaze in the rearview mirror, his expression stoic. "No."

Nathanial's nod was terse as he sat back and stared out the side window at the sparse landscape.

Audrey let out a silent huff. *Men.*

They arrived at a single dwelling with a detached garage on an acre lot. A large Christmas tree twinkled in the front window, and strands of colored lights hung from the eaves. As they parked in the driveway, the front door opened. A tall man with the same dark hair as Nathanial—only this man's was sprinkled with gray—stepped out of the house. He wore jeans and a thick sweater over wide shoulders. He squinted at them, no doubt wondering what the RCMP was doing at his house.

Audrey glanced from him to Nathanial and noted the striking resemblance between the two men. This had to be Nathanial's father.

"You ready for this?" she asked Nathanial.

He rolled his own wide shoulders. "I have to be." He caught her hand. "Would you mind saying a prayer?"

Surprised yet pleased by the request, she sought words. "Dear Lord, we come before You with humble hearts asking for clarity. We pray that Nathanial's mind will open up and remember his past. In Your name, amen."

"Amen," Nathanial murmured then gave her hand a squeeze. "Thank you. I can't express how glad I am that you're here. I don't think I could do this without you." He slipped his hand away and then stepped out of the truck.

Audrey swallowed back the pleasure of his words and fought for the emotional distance she knew she needed but was proving elusive.

Nathanial's heart pounded with trepidation. After the chaos of being chased and shot at, then coming face-to-face with a woman from his past, he was surprised by the depth of anxiety flooding his system.

Please, Lord, let me remember my father.

As he approached the man standing on the stoop, a glimmer of recognition ignited inside Nathanial's chest. There was no question in his mind that this man was his father. God was listening.

But Nathanial didn't know how to greet his dad. Were they the kind of people who hugged, or did they regulate their physical contact to a handshake?

"Son," the man boomed, his voice working its way through Nathanial to soothe away the worry. "What a nice surprise." He pulled Nathanial into his embrace. Nathanial breathed in the scent of pipe tobacco and pine. For a moment an image flashed of this man, his father, smoking a curled pipe near the fireplace, and a sense of security wrapped around Nathanial, much like the strong arms holding him close.

"Your mother will be giddy with joy." He released Nathanial and beamed at him. "She's at Coralie's having her
hair done. I'll give her a call."

"Thanks, Dad," Nathanial said, though the word felt
strange on his tongue. "But first I need to tell you something." He quickly explained about his memory loss, leaving out the attempts on his life. The last thing he needed to
do was upset his parents any more than he had to.

A frown deepened the lines around his father's light
brown eyes. "You don't know what happened to you?"

"No, but I'm hoping that being here will trigger my
memories." Feeling awkward, he gestured to his compan-
ions. "This is RCMP inspector Drew Kelley and his wife,
US FBI agent Sami Bennett-Kelley."

Dad shook hands with Drew. "I've heard about you,
Drew. I'm glad to meet you."

"Good stuff I hope, sir," Drew replied.

"Of course. And please, call me Leo."

Dad smiled at Sami and engulfed her hand in his large
one. "Welcome, Sami."

"Thank you, Leo," Sami replied.

"And this is Deputy Sheriff Audrey Martin." Nathanial
drew Audrey forward.

"A deputy." Curiosity radiated off Dad as he shook Audrey's offered hand. "It's nice to meet you."

"Likewise," Audrey said with a smile.

"Come in out of the cold." Dad led the way inside the
house and immediately went to the landline on the kitchen
counter to call his wife.

Nathanial remembered arguing with Dad about making sure he and Mom kept the landline despite the expense
when everyone they knew had converted to cell phones. In
case of an emergency at the house, the emergency response
dispatcher would immediately have their address to send

help, whereas a cell phone didn't provide the same sort of specific location, only a general area, which could take up precious time in getting rescue personnel to the scene.

Nathanial stepped inside, and a gush of emotion choked him. Sharp pain streaked through his head. He fought past it. "I do remember this place."

"That's good," Audrey said. "Just let your mind work at its own pace."

He nodded, knowing that every time he tried to force the memories to come, he only succeeded in causing himself pain. "Right."

He moved to the tree and touched the ornaments as more images rushed over him. The years of his childhood flooded in. Not all of them were happy memories. He closed his eyes, recalling the fights, the yelling between his parents and the scared little boy he'd once been, who'd hidden in the closet or under the covers of his bed to escape their furious voices.

An involuntary shudder rippled over him. Audrey touched his shoulder, her hand gentle but firm.

"Tell me what you remember," she said softly.

Sending a quick glance toward where his father spoke on the phone, Nathanial dropped his voice. "I don't think my parents' marriage is a happy one. They fought a lot."

Audrey's eyebrows rose. "But they're still together, so it couldn't be that bad."

She had a point. Something for him to ponder. Or ask his parents about. Later.

Dad hung up and joined them. "Your mom is on her way home. Can I offer you something to eat or drink?"

"Food would be great, Dad," Nathanial said, his mouth suddenly watering for a homemade meal.

Dad rubbed his hands together. "Perfect. I'll warm up your mother's split-pea soup and crusty bread."

"Thanks, Dad." Nathanial liked saying the word. It helped him to feel somewhat normal.

"Can we help?" Drew said, drawing Sami into the kitchen with Dad.

"Why don't you take a walk through the house, see what else you remember?" Audrey advised.

Nathanial headed down the narrow hallway with Audrey behind him. He stopped at the closed door of a room that had his name etched on a wooden plaque. His room. He pushed the door open, not sure what to expect.

Apparently his mother had turned his childhood space into her sewing area. A table with a large sewing machine was positioned beneath the overhead light. Knitting supplies spilled from woven baskets. Bolts of cloth and other paraphernalia were scattered around the floor.

A photo hung on the wall, drawing Nathanial's gaze. It was a family picture of his parents and him when he was around twelve. He held up a fish he'd apparently caught in the lake that provided a scenic backdrop. He touched the image of his mother. She was a beautiful woman with long straight black hair, black eyes that sparkled and a kind smile. They looked happy in this photo.

"You were a cute kid," Audrey commented as she moved to stand beside him.

"Thanks." The tantalizing scent of her vanilla shampoo teased his nose. He faced her. "What if that cute boy turned out to be a not-so-great guy?"

She tucked in her chin. "I don't believe that."

Needing an anchor, he fingered the silky strands of her hair.

It hurt his soul to think he'd been that guy.

Audrey placed a hand on his chest, over his heart. "We don't know all the details. You were both young. Don't condemn yourself without all the facts."

She always looked for the best in people and in situations. He was glad her time in law enforcement hadn't jaded her. "I admire how you keep giving me the benefit of the doubt," he said. "I don't think I deserve it."

"Everyone deserves the benefit of the doubt."

"Even a man who can't remember his past?"

"Especially a man who can't remember his past."

Attraction flared bright, like the North Star, guiding him toward her. She leaned closer as if she, too, were struck with the same powerful magnetic pull. His mouth hovered over hers, giving her a chance to back away. Her direct gaze welcomed him. He drew in a breath, prepared to follow through on the promised kiss.

"Nathanial!"

Audrey jerked back, disengaging from him in a split second. He closed his eyes for a moment as awareness and the most elemental memories washed over him. He recognized his mother's voice. He turned toward the woman who'd given birth to him with emotion choking the breath from his lungs.

Mom stood in the doorway, her face lit up with joy. She was about Audrey's height but slighter. Her long black hair was streaked with silver strands. Her blue pants were tucked into faux-fur winter boots. She wore a knitted sweater with a Christmas motif. She rushed forward to hug him.

"You've been gone too long," she breathed out.

"I'm here now." He held her tight as love swamped him.

She pulled back to look at him. "Your friends told your father you'd sustained an injury that put you in the hospital. You have amnesia?"

He told her of waking up on the beach in Calico Bay, not knowing how he had ended up there. "Audrey saved my life." His throat nearly closed on the words. His mom didn't seem to notice, but the quick look Audrey shot him made it clear she had. He quickly looked away before revealing how much she'd come to mean to him.

Mom captured Audrey's hands in hers. "Thank you."

"You're welcome." Audrey extracted her hands, her self-consciousness obvious only to him. "Is there a washroom available?"

"Across the hall," Mom said.

Left alone with his mom, Nathanial broached the subject of Laurie Bartlett. "What can you tell me about my relationship with her?"

Mom arched a black eyebrow. "What do you remember?"

"Nothing." He tried not to let frustration color his words. "We crossed paths with Laurie earlier today. She told me we were together for a while." And he'd seen the hurt in her eyes when she'd realized he didn't remember her. Had he broken her heart at one time?

Mom let out a long-suffering sigh. "She's a nice enough young lady. However, I never thought she was right for you. But what does a mother know?"

"Mom."

She patted his arm. "You two dated for most of high school and planned to get married the summer after you graduated."

"We didn't get married, though." Had he been commitment shy even then?

"No, you didn't."

Though he had no recollection of that time, something inside him reacted with a deep welling of sorrow that seared him in the heart. "Why didn't I marry her?"

"That's between you and Laurie."

Disappointed at the lack of information, he ran a hand through his hair. The sensation of guilt stole over him.

Had he callously ditched Laurie? Had he ever loved her? He needed to talk to her again. To know the truth, to make amends. "Have I been engaged to anyone else?"

"Not that I know of." Mom cupped his cheek. "I'm so proud of the man you've become."

He wished he could remember that man.

She linked her arm through his. "So tell me about Audrey."

"There's nothing to tell, Mom. She's helping me find my past." Because it was her job. But he wished it was so much more.

She patted his arm. "You keep telling yourself that."

TWELVE

Audrey closed the bathroom door behind her and pressed her hands to her hot cheeks, mortified that Nathanial's mother had nearly caught them in a kiss. Great, just the impression she wanted his family to have of her. Not. How totally unprofessional!

But she'd been unable to stop herself from offering Nathanial comfort. He was understandably upset over learning about his past relationship. Most likely Laurie had been his first love. But what had happened between them? "Lord, I'm not even sure what to pray. Healing, comfort? Forgiveness? You know what's needed."

Taking a breath to gain control of her emotions, she went in search of Nathanial and found him, his parents and the Kelleys seated at a round dining table. A hot bowl of soup and warm bread waited at the empty space next to Nathanial. She sat and ate the delicious food.

Mr. and Mrs. Longhorn regaled them with stories of Nathanial's childhood and teen years. Audrey liked the couple. They were so in sync with each other, often finishing each other's sentences and then laughing companionably. She wasn't sure what made Nathanial think his parents' marriage was less than happy. From her viewpoint they appeared to love each other deeply.

Audrey remembered what it had been like in her home before her father's death. Her mom and dad had been like the Longhorns, their love and affection evident in all they did. That wasn't to say Mom and Dad hadn't fought. They had. Mostly about Dad taking the boat out in too-rough water or during a storm. He'd always counter her arguments with the brief statement that he had to make a living and the fish didn't care what was going on above the water. Audrey knew her mother's objections stemmed from fear.

A fear that had come true when his boat had capsized during a raging storm. His body had never been recovered.

Nathanial nudged her with his knee, drawing her attention. "You okay?" he asked beneath his breath.

She sat up straighter. Letting melancholy drag her down and distract her focus wouldn't do. "Yes. I'm fine." To Mrs. Longhorn, she said, "This is the best soup I've tasted in a long time. Thank you."

"I'm so glad you're enjoying it," she replied.

When they were finished and had cleared the table, Sami drew Audrey aside.

"I think we should let Nathanial have some time with his parents alone," the FBI agent said. "He might remember more if we're not looking over his shoulder."

"I'm not comfortable leaving him here alone."

"We'll wait in the car."

Realizing Sami was right, Audrey grabbed her coat. She was prepared, after all, to do whatever necessary to help Nathanial fully regain his memory. Even if it was like pulling a fishhook from beneath her fingernail to let him out of her sight.

Nathanial watched the trio walk out the front door, leaving him with his mom and dad. As his parents had told stories of his past, he'd had flashes of memories that corresponded to their words. He sent up a silent prayer that his brain was healing and soon he'd regain all of his past, including the fateful day he'd disappeared from the rooftop in New Brunswick.

His mother hooked her arm through his and drew him to the couch. "I like your friends."

"Me, too. They're good people."

"Your grandmother will want to see you," Dad said as he took his seat in a leather chair facing the couch.

His grandmother. The word conjured up an image of an older version of his mother, with silver hair and a wreath of wrinkles around kind, laughing eyes. The ache of missing her clogged his throat. "I'll talk to the others about a visit."

"How long can you stay?" Mom asked.

"The night. The others have to get back to work, and I still have—" He stopped himself from revealing that someone was trying to kill him. He didn't want to worry them. "We're staying at the hotel on the edge of town."

"The Renners' place?" Dad asked.

"That's it."

"Nice people," Mom commented. "Do you remember Skip Renner? He was in your grade?"

He didn't. But he encouraged his parents to talk, to tell him more about his life. Though most of their stories weren't familiar, every once in a while he'd lock on a memory. Bits and pieces of his life took shape in his mind. There were still holes, and later that night after promising to swing by his parents' again in the morning before leaving, he lay in bed fitting the fragments together like a puzzle.

"Dear God, please help me to remember," he prayed in the dark hotel room. With Audrey next door and the Kelleys across the hall, Nathanial let his faith rise, hoping God would help him fill in the blanks.

But no matter how hard he concentrated on the one image connected to the mission that had gone so horribly wrong, his mind wouldn't move past that point of when he'd rolled over on that rooftop. He'd heard a noise from behind him. Something out of place. He was supposed to be alone. His heart hammered. He'd turned to face the threat...

Then nothing.

Always nothing.

He fell into a fitful sleep full of sinister figures that haunted his nightmares. And then there was Audrey banishing the shadows, offering him her hand, telling him it would be okay.

But would it? Would he ever remember? Or would he die first?

The next morning arrived with a swirl of fresh snow. Nathanial stepped out of the motel into the cold, tense with frustration and something else. A pending sense of doom that he'd awakened with and couldn't shake. As he waited for the others, he turned his face toward the sky and tiny flakes landed on his skin like kisses. He purposely relaxed his shoulders, but the unease clinging to him wouldn't release.

"You going to stick your tongue out and catch a snowflake?" Audrey asked with mirth lacing her tone.

Thankful for the distraction, he grinned at her and did just that.

She laughed, the sound cascading over him like sweet water, unaccountably smoothing away the frayed edges of his tension. An intense longing gripped him, making him want to whisk Audrey away, to go someplace where it was only the two of them. Somewhere the past didn't matter and no one was trying to kill him.

But he couldn't. The past did matter. He had to find the truth about it all.

And Audrey would never agree to shirk her responsibilities. He couldn't shirk his responsibilities. Nor could he ignore the guilt camping out in his chest. He had to know what he'd done to Laurie and apologize, though he doubted an apology would make up for whatever heartache he'd caused.

"I'd like to stop by Bartlett restaurant on the way to my grandmother's. I have to talk to Laurie again," Nathanial stated. "Apparently we were engaged once. I need to know what happened."

Audrey's blue eyes widened and then darkened with understanding. He could always count on her to comprehend doing the hard thing.

"I'll let the Kelleys know," she said, glancing at the motel entrance.

It wasn't long before the Kelleys walked out. Drew had his arm around Sami's shoulders. She smiled up at him with a heartfelt love shining on her pretty face. A twinge of something unfamiliar panged within Nathanial's heart. As they approached, he examined the feeling and realized with a start that it was envy.

He envied this couple their love, their togetherness. He wanted what they had with every fiber of his being. He almost let loose a laugh. Everything he'd heard about the man he'd been said he wasn't the type to settle down. Blake had made it clear he dated a lot but never got serious. Because of what happened with Laurie?

"I checked in with Director Moore," Drew said as he and Sami joined them near the SUV. "They received another tip that Kosloff is moving another shipment of arms north through the States. Blake and a team are going to intercept."

Nervous energy bounded through Nathanial. He wanted to join in the mission, to bring in Kosloff and make him tell them what had happened to Nathanial. But since that wasn't possible, he focused on clearing one aspect of his past at a time. He prayed Blake and the other IBETs team took Kosloff into custody.

"We'd like to stop by the Bartlett diner and grab breakfast," Audrey said.

Sami's eyebrows shot upward, and she pushed back a blond curl. "Okay. I could eat. And coffee would be welcome. But let's make it to go. I don't think we should linger."

Drew met Nathanial's gaze. "You sure?"

Nathanial nodded. "Very."

"All right. Load up." Drew climbed behind the wheel with Sami taking shotgun once again.

Audrey and Nathanial climbed into the borrowed RCMP SUV's back passenger seat. Heaviness pressed down on him. Was he doing the right thing by stopping there and wanting to talk to Laurie?

When they arrived at the restaurant, he hesitated. While Sami and Drew left the vehicle and headed inside, Audrey remained seated next to Nathanial.

"What do you hope to accomplish?" she asked. There was no judgment in her tone, only curiosity.

He told her what he'd learned last night from his mother. "I need to know why we broke up."

"Why?"

"I need to understand. To know what kind of man I am."

Audrey reached for his hand. "I don't think it matters who you were then as much as who you are now." She lowered her voice, and it seemed as if she struggled to say her next words. "I like the man you are now."

He curled his fingers around hers. "How is it that you always know the right things to say?"

"It's a gift." She extracted her hand and climbed out of the vehicle.

He followed her inside the eatery, the bells hanging on the door jangling. The place had just opened so they were the first customers of the day. And Sami and Drew had a booth by the front window, where they could keep watch in case a threat appeared. They joined them. An older woman came to take their orders. Her short dark hair framed an oval face that reminded Nathanial of Laurie. Her mother?

She eyed him with surprise. "Laurie mentioned you were home," she said with a smile. Her name tag read Martha.

"Is she here?" he asked. "I'd like to talk to her."

Creases appeared between Martha's eyebrows. "She's in the back. When I put your ticket in, I'll let her know you want to say hello."

"Thank you."

They each ordered breakfast to go, and then Martha headed to the kitchen. A few minutes later, Laurie walked out. She had an apron on over jeans and a long-sleeved T-shirt. Her dark hair was clipped back. Nathanial watched her approach and felt nothing. No stirring of attraction, no remembered intimacy. Nothing. She was a stranger to him.

She stopped beside their table. "Mom said you were asking for me."

"I'd like a moment of your time," he said and slid out of the booth. He gestured to the table a few feet away. "Can we sit?"

Her gaze settled on Audrey, who stared back at her with an implacable expression. Laurie finally nodded and moved to the table and sat. She folded her hands on the tabletop. "What is there to talk about? Are you still claiming amnesia?"

"Not claiming," he replied. Suddenly he wasn't sure if he wanted or needed to do this. What good would it accomplish? Knowing that he'd done this woman wrong would only eat at him. But he'd come this far; he had to see it through. He went for the heart of the matter. "We were going to get married. We didn't. Why?"

A pained expression marched across her face. His heart rate tripled.

"You don't remember the baby, either?"

He nearly choked. "I have a child?"

She shook her head. "No. I miscarried in the first trimester."

He tried to absorb her words. For a short time he'd been a father. He wasn't sure how to feel about that.

"You wanted to get married. You assumed because of the baby that was what we had to do," she continued softly.

Confusion reared up. "I don't understand," he said. "You didn't want to marry me?"

She lifted her chin. "Because of the baby I would have. But after...there was no point. I didn't love you. Not enough to spend the rest of my life with you."

He sat back as if someone had doused him with cold water, waking him up. Energy buzzed through his system. He wasn't sure how to process her words. "We must have had some feelings for each other if we made a baby."

She gave a dry chuckle. "Of course we did. We were seventeen and thought we were in love. But the reality of the baby and—" she waved a hand "—everything. It was too much for me. I couldn't handle it."

The guilt that had been slowly suffocating him let go. And he could breathe again.

"I know I hurt you." Guilt flashed across Laurie's face. "I'm sorry."

He felt almost giddy with relief. He hadn't dumped her. "I survived."

Though he couldn't remember the hurt, it didn't take a degree in psychology for him to comprehend the wound of her rejection had kept him from seeking love again. He'd used the rejection as an excuse to keep from committing. Because some part of him had understood that he didn't want to go through that kind of heartache again.

But was he willing to now? His gaze strayed to Audrey. She lifted her mug of coffee and met his gaze over the rim. He saw questions and concern in her pretty eyes.

She worried about him. He knew she didn't have to— he was in no danger at the moment—but still she cared. Warmth spread through his chest.

And he searched his own heart and found the answer to the question. Yes. He was willing to risk everything for his beautiful deputy. But would he? Did he have the guts? This trip home might not have accomplished the desired effect of regaining his memories, but he'd gained something else. His heart back.

Movement outside the window behind Audrey snagged his focus. A gold-colored luxury sedan pulled up near the front entrance. He recognized the car. And the three men exiting the vehicle, all dressed in dark clothes and hefting heavy artillery in their hands. Their faces and heads were uncovered, which didn't bode well.

Heart smashing against his breastbone, Nathanial jerked to his feet. "Kosloff's men."

Without hesitation Sami, Drew and Audrey scrambled out of the booth.

"Get the civilians out of here," Drew instructed as he drew his sidearm from the holster at his waist. He moved to a partition near the cash register where he'd have the tactical advantage when the men breached the front door.

The men outside let loose an onslaught of gunfire from automatic assault rifles that riddled the front of the restaurant with bullets.

"Hurry!" Sami waved the few waitstaff toward the kitchen. "Stay low." She hustled them out of harm's way while dialing for backup. Sami's voice sounded muffled in Nathanial's ringing ears.

"Go," he urged Laurie to follow Sami. Eyes wide with panic, Laurie jumped from her seat, toppling the chair in her haste to run to the back of the restaurant. The gunfire stopped.

Audrey rushed to Nathanial's side. "Let's get you somewhere safe."

"No." Nathanial resisted her prompting. He flipped the table over and they crouched down out of the line of sight behind it. "Do you have a backup piece on you?"

She hesitated for a fraction of a second before reaching for the small-caliber handgun holstered to her inner calf. She handed over the weapon. "We'll never win a shoot-out against their automatic weapons. We need to get out of here."

"We can't run," he said. He needed to end this. If they could capture one of the men and make him talk, then this nightmare could end. But it was a big *if*.

He put his hand on Audrey's shoulder. "Cover me."

Panic flared in her eyes. She opened her mouth to protest, but he was already moving toward the front door. He pressed his back on the opposite side from Drew. A busing cart rattled as Nathanial shoved it aside.

With jaw set, Audrey knelt behind the table, gripping her sidearm with two hands and keeping at the ready with the barrel aimed down but close to her chest. Her disapproving gaze burned through him.

Through the stuffy echo in his ears, Nathanial heard shouted commands.

"Send out Longhorn and no one else has to get hurt!" A heavily accented voice seeped beneath the front door. "We have the place surrounded. If we have to kill everyone, we will."

Nathanial met Audrey's gaze. She gave a vehement shake of her head.

He had no intention of dying today, but he also knew he couldn't let anything happen to his team or the innocent people in the kitchen. Slanting a glance at Drew, Nathanial wondered what he'd have done before losing his memories. Would he have given himself over for others, or would he have found a way to escape?

Leaving, saving his own hide, didn't sit well. In fact, the very thought was abhorrent to him. No way did he want to put others in unnecessary danger. "I'll come out, but you have to promise you'll let everyone else go."

"Dude," Drew barked at him. "We've seen their faces. They're not going to let any of us live."

"Sami is calling for backup. We have to stall for time," he insisted.

Audrey scrambled closer. "No way. As long as they stay outside, we can fend them off or pick them off if they enter. The RCMPs in Meadow Lake will arrive soon. I have to believe that. God won't let us die like this."

Her faith was strong and inspired him to hope she was right. He sent up a silent plea for help, for wisdom.

Screams from the kitchen jolted through him. Adrenaline spiked, making his blood freeze in his veins while his heart struggled to pump. What was happening?

"Sami!" Drew was across the diner before Nathanial could take a step.

The kitchen doors were kicked open. A man with a shaved head and dressed in camouflage clothes stepped into the dining room with an arm around Sami and a gun to her head. Drew halted abruptly. His shoulders heaved, and his fists clenched.

Audrey hissed in a shocked breath and aimed her weapon at the man.

"Put your weapons on the floor," the man said, his light eyes cold, devoid of emotion.

Nathanial held up his hands, showing the gun. "I'll go with you. Don't hurt anyone." As he slowly bent to place the gun on the floor, he bumped the busing cart. The rattle of utensils inside a plastic tub on the bottom shelf set off something inside him, but he didn't stop to think, he reacted. His hand reached into the tub and wrapped around the sharp blade of a steak knife. He met Sami's gaze, saw her fury but also saw the slight nod she gave him.

"Let me see your hands," the gunman barked.

Nathanial yelled, "Down."

Without hesitation, Sami went limp in her captor's arms, slipping from his grasp to the floor. As soon as she was clear, Nathanial, acting on some buried training, flung the steak knife. The blade hit its mark, embedding deep into the sinews and tendons of the bald thug's forearm. He screamed with pain and dropped his weapon.

Sami jumped to her feet and kicked the discarded rifle away as Drew lunged forward, seized the man and wrestled him to the ground, where he flipped the assailant onto his stomach and jammed a knee into his back. He took out a set of metal handcuffs and slapped them onto the thug's wrists.

Sami grabbed her weapon from the thug's waistband. "That's mine."

The bells over the door jingled as it opened. Drew and Sami took defensive positions.

Audrey swiveled toward the door. Two more gunmen stepped into the diner.

Terror smacked through Nathanial. No! Audrey was right in the line of fire.

Audrey squeezed the trigger of her sidearm, hitting the thug in front, who was shorter and broader than his cohort, in the leg. He went down, clutching his thigh.

The man's companion swung the barrel of his assault rifle toward Audrey.

Before the thug could pull the trigger, Nathanial tackled him, ramming the goon into the cash register counter. The guy was strong and wily. He pushed back from the counter, flinging his head back.

Agony vibrated down Nathanial's arm from the point of contact where the attacker's skull connected with his collarbone, but he fought through the glaring spots of pain to grasp the rifle, intent on gaining control of the weapon. They fell to the ground in a heap as they grappled for dominance.

Nathanial gritted his teeth with determination as he infused every ounce of power he had to wrest the rifle from the man's hands. The assailant's finger was on the trigger.

Boom.

THIRTEEN

The thunderous crack of several rounds exiting the assault rifle lodged between Nathanial and the assailant reverberated through Audrey, making her heart stall out with sudden fear.

Lord, please, no! I can't lose him.

The silent prayer screamed through her consciousness as plaster from the ceiling fell in bits and pieces. Her breath expanded in her chest as agonizing seconds ticked by. Was Nathanial hit? Was he alive? She refused to look too closely at the emotions welling up inside her.

Then Nathanial rolled away from the attacker, taking the rifle with him, and jumped to his feet in a defensive stance, ready to continue the fight. "Don't move!" he commanded the man on the ground. "Hands up where I can see them."

The man's sharp features reminded Audrey of a hawk—a beak of a nose, beady eyes and thin lips that twisted with rage—but he complied, slowly lifting his hands in the air.

Relief weakened Audrey's knees, but now wasn't the time to let down her guard. She quickly nudged both assailants' rifles to the side. Then, needing the action of cuffing the shorter man she'd shot as a way to distract herself from the rush of feelings flooding her heart, Audrey pulled the man's hands behind his back and encircled his wrists with a set of heavy-duty zip ties she'd pulled from her pants pocket. The smaller type of plastic ties could be easily broken, but these newer ones were more difficult for suspects to break. She handed Nathanial a second set.

"You've been carrying these around?" he asked as he took them and expertly secured hawk guy's hands behind his back.

"Of course," she said. "I may not be in uniform, but I'm always prepared."

"I like that about you," he said, his dark eyes holding hers with an intensity that had heat creeping up her neck.

Discomfited by his stare, she grabbed a cloth napkin and tied it around the wounded man's injury, then helped him to a sitting position next to the bald thug with his back resting against the booth bench.

"The civilians?" Drew asked Sami as he pulled her into his arms for a quick hug.

Seeing the couple together made Audrey's heart squeeze tight. She'd seen the panic and fear in Drew's eyes when Sami had been held captive, but he'd maintained his composure. She wasn't sure how. The man had a core of steel.

Her own heart had cramped when she realized Nathanial's intent. When he'd launched the steak knife, Audrey's mouth had dropped open in shock that had turned to awe when he'd disarmed Sami's assailant. How had Sami known Nathanial's aim would be true?

"They're safe," Sami replied to Drew's question about the restaurant's patrons and employees. "I had them squeeze into the pantry. I was coming back to help you when that one got the drop on me." There was no mistaking the bitter anger in her tone.

"My heart literally stopped beating," Drew said softly.

Sami leaned up to look into her husband's face. "Mine, too."

Seeing their obvious love for one another made Audrey's throat tighten. Longing for someone in her life with whom she could share that type of love and affection scraped along her nerves. Her glance slid to Nathanial. He watched her, his dark eyes unreadable.

Audrey dropped her gaze, her mind whirling. Earlier she'd feared for his life, and in that moment she'd realized she'd allowed herself to get too attached, too emotionally invested in Nathanial. Keeping him safe had become personal. Her feelings for him had become personal.

How could she let this happen? To cover her dismay, she busied herself by holstering her weapon. She had to stay focused on the job and keep her heart under better control.

Sami headed into the back to assure the civilians all was clear.

Drew hunched down in front of the two injured men. "Who sent you? How did you find us?"

Both men stared at him and remained mute.

Nathanial hauled the third attacker to his feet and pushed him to sit by his friends. "Why are you trying to kill me?"

The man sneered. He had deep-set eyes beneath thick brows. "You think you're safe. But you're not. None of us are."

Remembering what happened to the last thug they'd caught and questioned, Audrey said, "These men are in danger."

Nathanial glanced at her sharply. His eyes narrowed then widened with realization. "Right." He gave her an approving nod. "Their boss, Kosloff, will kill them for failing to do their job just like he did Sasha."

That got their attention. All three men reacted as if someone had poked them in the back with a sharp stick.

"That's right. We know who you work for," Nathanial said. "Tell me why Kosloff sent you and how you found us."

The bald thug laughed. "You think we know?" He had no discernible accent. Audrey figured the guy had to be American. "We do as we're told."

"You were told I'd be *here*?" Nathanial asked.

"We were told to watch for a RCMP vehicle and we'd find you," Baldy shrugged.

The answer oniy made Nathanial more convinced one of their own was working with Kosloff—how else would anyone know they'd changed vehicles? He discounted the Mounties they'd borrowed the SUV from because they'd had no clue Nathanial was headed here.

"Shut up," hawk guy barked in a heavily accented voice.

"You shut up!" Baldy shot back.

The screech of tires outside jolted an alert through Audrey. Doors slammed. Nathanial looked out the window. "The cavalry has arrived."

A moment later Inspector Cavendish stepped through the entrance, followed by two more Mounties with guns drawn.

"Well, seems you have everything under control here," Cavendish stated as he surveyed the scene.

"These two will need medical care," Audrey told him, pointing to the man she'd shot and the guy holding his arm where the steak knife had struck him, which was now wrapped with a blood-soaked cloth napkin. "The third guy is unharmed."

Cavendish nodded. "Thank you, Deputy Martin." He turned his attention to the three intruders. "I'm obligated to inform you of your right to counsel."

"We want to make a deal," hawk guy stated. "We'll tell you what we know for immunity."

"Which, apparently, isn't much, according to your friend," Audrey interjected.

Through the side window, Audrey observed the customers and employees leaving. She had no doubt Sami had taken their names and contact info for Inspector Cavendish to contact them later for statements.

"Not true," the man with the bullet in his leg said. He, too, had a thick Eastern European accent. "We have intel to trade."

The bald man smacked his accomplice. "No, we don't. Don't let them play you."

"No one is playing here," Drew stated in a deadly calm voice. "Tell us what we want to know. Make it easier on yourselves."

"Not without assurances," hawk guy said. "If we give you Kosloff's location, you let us walk."

Like that would happen. Audrey didn't blame the guy for trying, but he wouldn't be skating on attempted murder. The best he and his associates could hope for were reduced sentences.

Bald guy groaned. "We're dead. Kosloff's spies are everywhere."

"We can talk to the minister of justice," Inspector Cavendish said. "But it's up to the minister's judgment." He nodded to his sergeants. "Take them into custody. We'll hold them at the station until the crown attorney can be dispatched from Regina."

After they were gone, Nathanial slammed a fist on the table. "We have to find Kosloff. I can't keep living like this. I have to know what happened."

Wincing at his pain, Audrey wished there was a way she could help him. But she had no idea how. Returning to his hometown and seeing his parents hadn't dislodged the crucial memory of what happened to him. "We should go where you were last before losing your memory." She prayed that would be the catalyst to bring back the events of that day.

"Good idea," Drew said. "Maybe on that rooftop you'll remember."

Nathanial ran a hand through his dark hair. "It certainly couldn't hurt."

"I'll call Blake and let him know where we're going," Drew said, taking out his cell phone.

Sami followed her husband outside to the borrowed RCMP vehicle.

The desolate expression on Nathanial's face made Audrey's heart twist. She went to his side and put a hand on his shoulder. "You okay?"

"Not really." He took her hand in his. "Everywhere I go, death and destruction seem to follow me." He let out a mirthless laugh. "Merry Christmas."

His sarcasm echoed through the empty restaurant. Audrey moved to stand in front of him, forcing him to meet her gaze. "Look. This isn't your fault. We'll get the man responsible. You have to believe that."

He frowned. "I do. I know eventually the IBETs team will take down Kosloff and whoever is working for him."

"And you'll be with your team."

"Maybe."

A noise near the kitchen door sent alarm exploding inside Audrey. She spun toward the sound while reaching for her weapon. Nathanial stepped in front of her as a shield. Even as it registered what he was doing, Audrey's heart melted a little. Strangely she wasn't irritated by his move, as she normally would be if any other man had thought she needed to be protected.

With Nathanial, she knew it wasn't a power play but his natural instinct to guard, to protect. To show he cared.

Laurie stood in the doorway, frozen. Her brown eyes were large and scared. A visible tremor ran through her. "Sorry. Didn't mean to startle you."

Taking a calming breath, Audrey relaxed her stance and dropped her empty hands to her sides.

"Laurie, I thought you left with your mother," Nathanial said but didn't move toward her.

"I came back to see if you were still here," Laurie replied. She took a deep breath and squared her shoulders as if bracing for battle.

Audrey pressed her lips together. Did the woman hope to reclaim him? Why did that thought make Audrey's blood pressure rise? It wasn't as if she and Nathanial were a couple. They worked together for now, but that was all.

Yet she couldn't help the thrum of possessiveness that ran a ragged course through her. She purposely stepped back as if somehow putting distance between herself and Nathanial could control her feelings. Feelings that were simmering below the surface and threatening to boil over. Feelings she didn't want to name or look at too closely. Her pulse ticked up.

Nathanial slanted a curious glance at Audrey, and she was careful to keep her expression neutral so he wouldn't see what was bubbling inside her.

"We were just heading out," Nathanial replied to Laurie. "I'm sorry for what happened today. I shouldn't have come here."

Laurie stepped closer. "I wanted to make sure you were okay. That you don't...still hate me."

Audrey cocked her head and stared at the pair. Hate her? What had happened between them? Curiosity burned beneath her breastbone, and she absently rubbed at the spot.

It didn't matter. It wasn't her concern. She had no right to wonder, let alone ask. But knowing that didn't squelch her interest.

"I'm good," he said. "I don't hate you." He grimaced. "The past is gone for me. I may never remember." He took a shuddering breath. "I'm glad you told me, though. It helps to know." He took her hand. "I hope that you find happiness."

A tentative smile spread over her face. "Thank you." Her gaze jumped to Audrey then back to him. "I hope you do as well." He dropped her hand, and she turned to leave the way she'd come in. "Goodbye."

"Goodbye, Laurie." Nathanial put his hand to the small of Audrey's back and ushered her out the restaurant's front entrance.

Giving in to the curiosity itching at her, she peered at him. "What was that about?"

"Putting the past to rest," he murmured as he led her to the vehicle, keeping her from asking any more questions.

Drew hung up from his call. "Blake and the team will meet us in New Brunswick."

"Great." Nathanial opened the back passenger door for Audrey. "Let's pray I can recall something that will put an end to this nightmare."

The trip from Saskatoon to Saint John, New Brunswick, took three plane changes. On the first leg Nathanial was too keyed up to rest, but Audrey slept. When her head bobbed for the third time, he'd gently positioned her so that she pressed against his arm and her head rested on his shoulder. The fragrance of the hotel shampoo clinging to her hair teased his nose, but the subtle scent that was completely hers, and hers alone, filled his senses.

Tender affection invaded his chest, clutching his heart

in a fierce grip. He didn't know why God had allowed this amazing woman to be the one to find him on the beach, but he was grateful nonetheless. There was something about her that called to something deep inside him. He couldn't say if he'd ever felt this way before, and the feeling was strange and wonderful all at once.

He called himself all kinds of a fool for letting himself become attached to the lovely Audrey, but how could he not? She was a treasure. And the fact that some jerk had abused her trust and love made Nathanial's blood boil and his heart hurt.

When they landed in Winnipeg, Audrey awoke. She jerked upright as if stunned to find she'd been leaning on him. "Ugh. Did I drool?"

He chuckled. "Not that I noticed."

She busied herself gathering her belongings, but there was no hiding the blush raging on her fair cheeks.

They disembarked and met Drew and Sami for a quick bite to eat before boarding the next plane. On the second leg of the trip, he finally succumbed to exhaustion. He awoke as the captain was announcing their descent into Toronto. He lifted his head from Audrey's shoulder and grinned. "Did I drool?"

She laughed, her blue eyes sparkling despite the dim lights of the plane's interior. "Like a hound dog."

He wiped his mouth and flushed with embarrassment. "Sorry."

"I'm joking," she said.

"Good. I'd hate to have you think I'm a Neanderthal."

She scrunched up her nose. "Never."

This time when they disembarked, they had to hustle to their next gate to make the last leg of the trip to Saint John. Audrey and Nathanial sat together again with Sami and Drew in the row behind them. Night had fallen long ago. Outside the airplane's small oval windows lay a vast darkness.

Since they both had slept, they were both wide-awake. Nathanial could tell Audrey had something on her mind because she kept sending him sideways glances, and her bottom teeth tugged on her lower lip. He'd seen her nervous, irritated and determined, but not uncertain. And it made him nervous. When she started picking at a hangnail, he finally reached over and covered her hands.

"What is it?" he asked.

Her eyebrows rose. "What do you mean?"

"You're fidgeting. Something has you twisted up inside. Maybe I can help?" He'd like to do whatever he could to repay her for all she'd done for him.

She made a face. "I didn't realize I was that transparent. I keep telling myself it's none of my business, but…"

"But?"

"What happened between you and Laurie? What did she say when you two talked?"

Ah. He should have known she'd wonder. Who wouldn't? He thought about how best to answer. Straightforward was the best and only approach. "Apparently whatever we had was one-sided." He told her the gist of his past with Laurie. "She only agreed to marry me because of the baby. Afterward, she rejected me."

Audrey's mouth formed an O. "I see. The decisions we make when we're young can haunt us the rest of our lives."

He let out a dry laugh. "If one can remember them."

Audrey's steady gaze held. A man could happily drown in those blue pools. "You can't give up hope that you'll remember."

Her optimism was endearing. "From what I've gleaned from Blake and Drew, I haven't let myself fall in love again."

"Understandable. She broke your heart."

He shrugged. He couldn't remember, but if Laurie had thought he was mad at her because she'd turned down his offer of marriage, then maybe she *had* broken his heart. Or at least made him wary of relationships. He surely never wanted to compromise his faith again. "All I know for sure is that the future looks so much brighter than it did."

A shadow crossed her face. "That's good."

She hadn't healed from the wound inflicted by her college love. "Do you trust me?"

She tucked in her chin and eyed him warily. "Yes."

He gave her his most dazzling smile. "Even if I'm charming?"

With a roll of her eyes, she shook her head. "Don't let it go to your head."

He chuckled then sobered. "I'm serious. I hope you won't let your past hurtful relationship keep *you* from finding love."

"It's not just Kyle that has held me back," she admitted softly. "I have dated since Kyle. Most men are either intimidated by me or want to change me into something I'm not."

"So you mentioned." It pained him to think she'd been treated poorly and made to feel bad about herself. "I like you, Audrey. A lot. Just as you are."

For a brief second, pleasure flared in her eyes, then she dropped her gaze to their entwined hands. Slowly she extracted her hand from his grasp. "Thank you for saying that. I like you, too, Nathanial. You're a good man."

He could feel her withdrawing from him emotionally as well as physically. It stung more than it should. "I hear a *but* in there."

She sat up straighter. "No *but*."

Hmm. Okay. Then why did he feel disappointed—let down, even?

They sat in silence the rest of the flight. It was nearly three in the morning when they touched down in Saint John. Blake was waiting for them at the curb outside the airport. The temperature was below freezing. Ice crusted on the walkway and road. Nathanial was thankful he'd grabbed a down jacket, wool cap and gloves from his parents' house. They piled into a warm minivan.

Blake drove them to a hotel and handed out key cards. "We'll meet back in the lobby in four hours."

Nathanial was grateful for the opportunity to shower and change clothes. He tried relaxing by stretching out on top of the bed but was too restless. He watched the minutes tick by on the clock. Finally it was time to leave his room. He opened the door to find Audrey about to knock.

"Couldn't sleep, either?" he asked as he closed the door behind him.

She gave him a wry smile. "No."

They met the others in the lobby, and Blake drove them to the warehouse district where their mission had gone wrong. A dozen men waited for them at the entrance to a redbrick building.

Nathanial scanned the faces of the men, hoping for some hint of recognition, and found none.

"Where's Chase?" Blake asked one of the men.

"Not sure. I would have thought he'd beat us here, since he was nearby following up on a lead," the man said, his badge identifying him as Agent Phillips of the Immigration and Customs Enforcement agency, like Blake.

"And Luke?" Drew asked.

"No sign of the border patrol guy, either," ICE agent Phillips stated.

A man came running up. His jacket had the RCMP logo on the breast pocket. "Inspector Kelley!"

"What is it, Sergeant?" Drew peered at the younger Mountie.

The sergeant pointed down the block. "I was doing a perimeter sweep as Agent Phillips asked when I came across an abandoned SUV. There's signs of a struggle. And blood."

FOURTEEN

"That doesn't sound good," Audrey said beneath her breath to Nathanial. She had a bad feeling about this. Two agents were missing. And there was blood at the scene of one agent's abandoned vehicle. She shivered at the implications. If someone in their ranks was working for Kosloff, they could all be walking into a trap. "We need to leave."

Nathanial shook his head. "We've come this far—we can't give up yet. I have to try."

She understood his need to recall what had transpired on the roof of this building. She glanced around, seeing the swarm of agents and officers from both sides of the international boundary line. There was tension etched on each person's face. They, too, felt exposed, vulnerable. She moved closer to Nathanial with her hand on her weapon. He was a target, and a kill shot could come from any of the rooftops or cars parked along the street. She met Sami's gaze and saw the worry in her eyes. Audrey turned back to Nathanial. "The risk is too great."

"Not your call, Deputy Martin," he said in a firm, impersonal tone that bit into her. To Blake he said, "I'm going up while you search for Luke and Chase."

"We're coming with you," Drew stated. Sami nodded her agreement.

Audrey thrummed with frustration. However, she had no choice but to go with Nathanial as he headed inside the large four-story brick building. Aggravated by his bullheadedness, she sent up a quick prayer for protection and hustled after him.

At one time the large building had housed the offices of a shipping conglomerate, but it had long been abandoned, like so many older buildings in the area. The place smelled musty with disuse. Office windows were missing; doors hung on broken hinges. Chunks of plaster had fallen from the ceiling where water damage had seeped into the structure. She hurried by Nathanial to take the lead. She didn't miss the wry twist of his lips. Thankfully he didn't argue. Drew and Sami took the rear position.

Audrey held her sidearm in a two-handed grip as they stepped into a rickety elevator, which took them to the top floor. From there they had to take a steep flight of stairs to the roof. At the door to the rooftop, she paused, putting her hand out for Nathanial to wait as she eased the door open and peered out, bracing herself in case they came upon a hostile.

The roof appeared clear. She pushed the door wider and stepped out into the overcast morning. Wind whipped across the roof, stirring up debris. There was no one on the roof.

Nathanial nudged her aside. "I would have been positioned there." He pointed to the southeast corner that faced the warehouse where the raid on Kosloff had been scheduled to take place.

"That's right," Drew confirmed. "That's where we found your discarded hardware."

"Were there signs of a struggle?" Audrey asked.

"The crime scene techs found one drop of blood," Drew

told them. "We had it DNA tested, and it was a match to you."

"The blow to his head happened here, then," she said, trying to envision the scene. "He was lying there, facing the street. He'd have been vulnerable to an attack from behind."

"I was struck on the left side of my head," Nathanial said, his dark eyes taking on a faraway look. He rubbed his forehead; no doubt another headache was taking hold of him.

She hated that he had to go through this pain. "The perp struck him, then stripped him of his accoutrements, leaving them behind for his team to find. Why not take them?"

"Good question. If it was one of Kosloff's goons, one would think they would want the flak vest and the weapons," Drew stated.

"Or they didn't want to risk being seen with my equipment. Too identifiable." Nathanial moved toward the edge of the roof.

"Which takes us back to the idea it was an insider. Someone who needed his cover to stay intact." She stuck to Nathanial's side, her gaze alert for any sign of danger. Drew followed while Sami monitored the door in case someone tried to come through and catch them from behind.

Nathanial lay down and mimed the action of looking through a rifle scope. "I had a clear view of the warehouse," he said. "And of the neighborhood."

"A car turned on the street a few blocks down to the right," Drew said.

Nathanial shifted his attention to where Drew indicated.

"Tell us about the car," Audrey said.

"A black sedan with tinted windows," Drew supplied. "It rolled down the street slowly. Nathanial must have seen it, because he said to hold. We all held our positions, waiting for more info. None came. Two ATF agents approached the car and were fired upon."

"And killed." There was no mistaking the note of self-incrimination in Nathanial's tone.

Audrey hurt for him. "By then you were already out of commission. It's not your fault."

He glanced over his shoulder. Frowned, then rolled onto his back. Shielding his eyes from the overcast sun's glare with his hand, he said, "Step closer."

She did as he asked, casting a shadow over him. "What is it?"

Without answering, he moved onto his stomach and sighted the warehouse with his hands. He closed his eyes, then suddenly turned over onto his back to stare up at her. He blinked and then sat up abruptly. "I never saw my attacker's face."

Surprise washed through Audrey. "You can't identify him?" That was good news, wasn't it? Then why did Nathanial seem upset?

Nathanial shook his head with frustration. He'd so wanted to be able to proclaim the name of the man who'd assaulted him and thrown him into the ocean in the hopes he'd die. And was still trying to do him in. "No. He'd have been standing where you are with the sun at his back. All I would have seen was the dark outline of his body."

"The person trying to kill you doesn't know that. He fears you'll be able to identify him if you regain your memory," Audrey said with excitement in her voice. "We have to get this news out there so he'll stop coming after you."

"No." Nathanial rose to his feet. His head pounded, but he ignored the throbbing ache. "We have to catch the perpetrator. Whoever attacked me is working for Kosloff. If we can draw the suspect out into the open, then maybe we can capture him and use him to get Kosloff."

"That sounds risky," Audrey said.

"No more risky than letting him off the hook so he can continue to put other lives in jeopardy," he countered.

She pressed her lips together. As an officer of the law, he knew she couldn't refute his logic. But she wanted to. He could see it in the worry darkening her blue eyes.

"Maybe we need to start looking at how you ended up in the ocean," she said. "You were knocked unconscious here. The guy would have had to carry you out of the building and put you in a vehicle."

"We need to know where every agent and officer was at the time," Nathanial said. "Someone had to have seen something."

"Let's go confer with Blake," Drew instructed. "He'll have the schematics of the operation."

"It would also be helpful to learn if you were dropped into the ocean from shore or a boat," Audrey said as they walked toward Sami, where she stood waiting by the stairwell door. "If you were taken out on a boat, which seems most likely, we could look at all the harbors to see if we can find video-surveillance cameras."

"Good idea. Director Moore has been in contact with the New Brunswick authorities, requesting security videos in a ten-block radius from here," Sami said. "We're still waiting for them. I'll add the harbors to the request." Her curious gaze shifted to Nathanial. "Did you remember something?"

His gut churned with failure. "Unfortunately, no. This trip was a bust."

Audrey arched an eyebrow at Nathanial. "That's not really correct. You may not have remembered what happened, but we know what you didn't see."

He shrugged. She tended to see the bright side of things. To him, they were no better off than before coming to the roof. He wished he were more like Audrey. "True, but that doesn't get us any closer to taking down Kosloff and finding out who tipped him off to the raid. Besides, there may still be some memory of seeing my attacker locked in my brain."

"What happened?" Sami asked.

Drew quickly explained as they entered the stairwell. Their footsteps echoed off the concrete walls.

"Ah, I can see how that would be frustrating," Sami said.

They stepped into the elevator, and the doors slid shut. Drew pushed the button for the first floor. The car moved with a groan. A few seconds later, it jolted to an abrupt stop.

Nathanial jabbed a finger at the elevator car panel. Nothing worked. The doors remained closed. They moved neither up nor down. He wasn't sure if they were between floors or not.

Drew opened the call box. At one time it held a receiver connected to a security office in the building. But both were gone now.

Audrey checked her phone. "No bars."

"Me, either," said Drew as he looked at his cell phone.

A thud sounded on the ceiling.

Audrey reached for her weapon and gripped Nathanial's arm. His heart beat in his ears. Was someone up there? Had someone dropped something on the top of the elevator? If so, what?

A scraping noise echoed inside the elevator car, tightening his nerves. The emergency panel in the ceiling shifted slightly to allow a small tube to dangle into the car. Someone was up there!

"What is that?" Sami asked.

"It looks like a hose," Audrey replied.

"That's exactly what it is," Nathanial said. A wave of apprehension crashed over him as a hissing sound came from the hose. "Cover your mouths and noses!"

The compartment filled with a toxic gas that stung his eyes. Panic revved through his blood. Audrey jumped and batted at the hose with her free hand while her other hand covered her mouth and nose, trying unsuccessfully to push the hose out of the opening.

Nathanial took shallow breaths and attacked the elevator door. His muscles strained as he dug his fingers into the crevice where the doors met. Drew crowded in to help.

With their combined strength, they managed to inch the two sides apart, enough to let in some fresher air. They were between the floors. Nathanial could see the cables and stone wall outside the elevator.

"Sami!" Audrey's cry jerked Nathanial's attention to the FBI agent. She was slumped on the floor, having succumbed to the gas.

Drew shoved the two sides of the door farther apart. "We have to get out of here."

Nathanial reached out and grabbed a set of cables. Hand over hand he shimmied up the cables until he could see the top of the elevator car. A black hose connected to a canister sat on top. The doors to the building were open. A black shadow appeared. Not a shadow—a man dressed all in black. He aimed an assault rifle at Nathanial.

His heart stalled. He had nowhere to hide.

The emergency panel in the elevator car ceiling flipped up, knocking the canister over. Audrey crawled out of the opening, quickly pushing the offending hose aside.

"Watch out!" Nathanial warned. "Shooter in the doorway."

Audrey reached up with her sidearm and fired at the

man. The man dived out of the way, and the bullet hit the metal side of the door.

Audrey's panic-filled gaze jerked to Nathanial. "You okay?"

"Yes." He swung his feet to the top of the elevator car. Inside the car, Drew held Sami in his arms.

"You help them up," Audrey instructed. Before he could protest, she rose and in one graceful move, reached for the doorsill and muscled her way to the floor. She rolled out of sight with her gun at the ready.

Terrified something would happen to her, Nathanial had to force himself not to follow her. Sami and Drew needed his help. He sent up a silent plea for God to keep her safe. To protect her, to bring her back to him.

He reached into the elevator car as Drew hefted Sami's petite, unconscious frame up. Nathanial caught her under the arms and dragged her as gently as he could out of the elevator. Then Drew jumped up, catching the lip of the opening, and pulled himself out of the car. Nathanial gripped the doorsill, much like Audrey had, and climbed out of the elevator shaft. He pressed his back to the side panel and peered around the edge. The hallway was empty. He quickly helped Drew with Sami. Once they were all out, Drew lifted Sami in his arms. "We have to find the stairs. She needs a medic."

Nathanial looked at Drew. "Let me have your weapon."

Drew didn't hesitate. "Take it."

Withdrawing Drew's sidearm from his holster, Nathanial led the way into the darkened interior in search of the stairwell. "Audrey?" he called out.

Nothing.

Where could she be? He prayed for her safety. They came to a corner in the hallway. He held up his hand to indicate to Drew to halt. He peered around the corner. A door opened at the far end of the hall. He lifted Drew's Glock. A figure stepped out of the stairwell. A shaft of gray light shone on blond hair. Audrey. He lowered his weapon with an exhale of relief. He called out her name.

She hustled toward him. "Suspect got away. I chased him down the stairs that lead to the back alley. By the time I reached the bottom, he was nowhere to be seen."

Drew rounded the corner with Sami held close to his chest. They hurried down the stairs and out the building's back exit. They moved swiftly down the alley and around to the front where the IBETs team waited. Blake paced with his cell phone pressed to his ear. When he saw them, his eyes widened and he hung up. Nathanial tucked Drew's gun into the waistband of his jeans.

"What happened?" Blake's concern shone on his face.

"We need an ambulance." Audrey explained what had transpired.

Blake's eyes darkened with anger. "How could this happen?" He barked out orders for other agents to secure the building and call in the crime-scene technicians.

Drew sat on the tailgate of an SUV with Sami secure in his arms. She'd awakened but still appeared weak from the gas.

Nathanial cupped Audrey's elbow and tugged her out of earshot of the others. "You shouldn't have taken off like that."

"Excuse me?" She drew back from him. "One of us had to go after the perp."

She was right and he knew it, yet he couldn't shake the dread that had taken up residence in the middle of his chest. If something had happened to her...

He couldn't bear the thought. Wow. He had it bad. And she wasn't the one who wanted or needed protection, but he couldn't help feeling protective. He was letting his feelings for her affect his judgment. He needed to put some distance between them, to give himself some space to figure out exactly what he felt for her.

And then he'd have to decide what to do about it.

Audrey tamped down the irritation crawling up her neck as she watched Nathanial striding away. He stopped to check on the Kelleys. She knew Nathanial well enough to know he wanted to protect her. He was that kind of guy. Protecting others was second nature to him. But she was a deputy sheriff, and running toward danger was a part of her.

For as long as she could remember, she'd been the one to step in to break up fights on the school yard, the first one to defuse volatile situations. Going into law enforcement had fit perfectly with her personality. She was good at her job. And if Nathanial couldn't see or accept that, then there was no future for them.

Her stomach knotted. Future? With Nathanial?

Did she want one? Her heart rate ticked up, and she took an involuntary step back. Maybe. She didn't know. There was still so much unresolved in his life. And there were issues she needed to face. Like did she trust him not to break her heart?

That was a no-brainer. Of course she did. He was a man of integrity and honor. But what would she have to give up to forge a life with him?

Her job? Her plans to become sheriff? Her country?

Much more than she was willing to sacrifice. No. A future with Nathanial wasn't possible. More than a boundary line separated their lives.

The jangle of her cell phone was a welcome distraction. She glanced at the screen. Her mom. No doubt Mom was wondering where she was and if she were okay. Audrey hadn't checked in for a few days. She pressed the talk button.

"Hi, Mom."

"Listen carefully and don't say a word," a man's deep voice intoned into Audrey's ear.

Her stomach dropped, as if the earth had given way beneath her feet. Her hand tightened around the phone pressed to her ear.

"If you want to see your mother alive again, you bring Longhorn to her cottage. You tell anyone, and I'll know. And then your mother will die."

The caller clicked off. Silence echoed inside her head.

Her mother was being held hostage.

By a man whose voice Audrey recognized.

FIFTEEN

"We can reconvene at the IBETs headquarters," Blake said. "I don't want to conduct interrogations out in the field. I'll need to study the schematic to ascertain those who would have been in position to have a clear view of the back alley."

Nathanial wanted answers now but understood Blake's concern. Questioning the other officers and agents on the fly could lead to confusion and show their hand before they were ready. "Any word on Chase or Luke?"

Bleakness entered Blake's eyes. "No. Nothing. No trace of where they are or what happened to them."

"We have to check the docks." Nathanial hated to think that the two men were floating in the ocean as he'd been. Thankfully he'd washed ashore and had been rescued by a beautiful golden-haired deputy.

He could only pray Chase and Luke were as equally blessed to not only survive but be rescued.

Though he doubted anyone could top Audrey as a rescuer. His gaze slid to where she stood on the sidewalk next to the building with her phone in her hand. Though the day was overcast, her blond hair brightened up the gloomy weather.

But her pale, stunned expression wasn't what he'd expected to see. His stomach lurched. Something was wrong. He hurried to her side.

"Audrey?"

She lifted her blue gaze to his as she disconnected the call. Her pupils were blown wide. Her breathing came in small gasps. "They have my mom."

"What? Who?" He gripped her shoulders. "Talk to me."

She shook her head. "Not here. Will you come home with me?"

He tilted his head. "Tell me what's happening. How can I help if I don't know what's wrong? Who is *they*?"

Her gaze darted left and right as if afraid someone would overhear their conversation. "It's not safe to talk here."

Grabbing his arm, she tugged him into the shadows between two buildings. "I received a call from my mom's phone. Only it wasn't her. The man on the other end said he'd kill her if I don't bring you to the cottage."

The air swooshed out of his lungs. *Will you come home with me?* Did she mean to trade him for her mom? No. She wouldn't do that. She wanted his help. There was no mistaking the pleading in her eyes. It took a second for him to catch his breath. "Let's not panic. We'll get Drew and Blake and head to Calico Bay."

"No." She clutched at his arm. "He said we had to come alone."

"They always say that," he said.

"Listen to me," she demanded. "He said he'd know if we told anyone."

Nathanial frowned. "Did he identify himself?"

"He didn't have to," she said, her voice shaking. "I know who it is. I know who betrayed you."

He stilled as alertness stole over him. "What are you saying?"

"Nathanial, it was Chase."

He rocked back as if someone had slapped him. "Wait. You're saying *Chase* is the one who called you threatening your mother?"

"It was him. I'm certain. He's the one working for Kosloff."

Nathanial reeled from the news. That day in the sheriff's office had been a charade—Chase's show of rage and grief, blaming Nathanial for two deaths, had been an act, and he'd had his own men killed. Had he been the man on the rooftop? The man who'd repeatedly tried to kill Nathanial?

"We have to tell Blake," Nathanial insisted. "We'll leave the Kelleys out of it. Thanks to the toxic gas, Sami's in no condition to deal with this. And we're going to need help to get your mother back."

Audrey took a shuddering breath. "I agree. My great-uncle and the others will help us. But I'm not sure telling Blake is a good idea. If Chase has more traitors working with the IBETs team, he'll know if we talk."

Nathanial shoved a hand through his hair. "We have to get Blake away from here so we can talk to him."

"How?"

"I'll tell him my head is killing me," he said, which wasn't too far from the truth. He indeed had a splitting headache. "I'll ask him to take us to the hotel. We'll explain on the way."

"What if…if he's with Kosloff? He and Chase seemed tight."

Nathanial's mind rebelled at the thought of Blake being dirty. No way. He took Audrey's hands in his. "We have to trust someone. Everything inside me says Blake is a stand-up guy."

"I'm sure everyone thinks the same of Chase."

She had a point. But they needed assistance getting back

to Calico Bay. Not to mention support, weapons, ammu-
nition and manpower. Yes, Sheriff Crump and his deputies would be useful, but Nathanial doubted they had the
experience to tackle a situation like this one.

The photo from Blake's wedding surfaced in Nathanial's mind. He'd trusted Blake in the past. He had to put
his life, and those of Audrey and her mother, in his hands
now. It would take a leap of faith. "Pray with me," he said
to Audrey. "Pray that God will guide us and guard us and
your mother."

She nodded and tugged him closer. "Dear Father in
Heaven, please hear our prayer. We ask for Your wisdom,
Your guidance and safety for my mom. For us as we res-
cue her."

Nathanial nodded his agreement and gave her a reassuring smile that they would succeed in rescuing her mother.
Now that they knew who the bad guy was, they could put
an end to this nightmare.

They found Blake giving orders to pack up and return
to the IBETs headquarters in Washington, DC.

"Hey," Blake said as they halted at his side. "We're
heading out. I'll have Phillips drive you to the hotel to pick
up your stuff and then take you to the airport."

"No," Nathanial said. "We need to go with you."

He frowned. "I'm staying to wait for the crime-scene
techs."

"Let Phillips do that," Nathanial said, holding his gaze
steady and trying to convey the necessity through his stare.
"We need you to take us to the airport. It's important."

Blake cocked his head then nodded slowly. "Okay."

Nathanial was a bit surprised by Blake's easy accep-
tance and grateful for it as well. He and Audrey climbed
into the black SUV to wait for Blake as he gave Agent
Phillips instructions. A few moments later, Blake joined

them in the vehicle and slid behind the steering wheel. He remained silent as he fired up the engine and drove away from the harbor area.

"Explain," he said finally.

Nathanial nodded to Audrey. This was her story to tell. She quickly laid out the details of the call.

Blake pulled the SUV to the side of the road. "Let me get this straight. ATF agent Chase Smith is involved with Kosloff? He's holding your mother hostage?"

"Yes." Nathanial felt Blake's upset all the way to the soles of his feet. "It's mind-blowing."

"It's ridiculous," Blake stated.

"I know it was him on the phone," Audrey insisted. Nathanial folded his hand over hers, offering her his support. He believed her.

Blake started driving again. "We'll find out soon enough."

Two and half hours later, they rolled into Calico Bay. The sky was clear. Clumps of snow lined the streets. The Christmas decorations on the storefronts were a mockery of the anxiety filling Nathanial as they halted in the back parking lot of the sheriff's department.

The last time Nathanial had been here, the generator had blown up and men with guns had tried to kill him. He'd survived thanks to the woman at his side. Their trek through the tunnels to the cliffs would forever be ingrained on his brain.

Audrey jumped out and hurried inside the station. Nathanial and Blake followed in her wake. Before stepping inside, Blake put a hand on Nathanial's arm, halting him. "You trust this woman?"

"Funny, she asked me the same thing about you." Nathanial stared at the man he'd once called friend. "I trust her with my life. Just as I'm trusting you with all of our lives."

An interesting array of emotions crossed Blake's face. "When this is over, you have to come to Hilton Head. Liz will want a full accounting and to make sure for herself you're okay."

"Sounds like a plan." He took a deep breath and slowly let it out. "But first let's put an end to this ordeal. Kosloff and his minions are going down."

Nervous energy buzzed through Audrey's body, making it difficult for her to concentrate. A state she'd never experienced before. Nothing had prepared her for the fear of losing her mother to some psychotic rogue ATF agent and his Russian arms-dealer boss. She paced a short path inside her great-uncle's office as he, Nathanial and Blake strategized how best to execute a rescue of her mother. She listened, but her heart was busy praying.

She'd never had her faith tested so greatly before. She wanted to rail at the sky, shake her fist and ask God why He'd allow her mother to be put in such a dangerous situation.

But Audrey knew that God wasn't at fault. He gave men free will to do good and evil. But God also gave strength and protection to His people.

She clung to the verse running through her head. *Have I not commanded you? Be strong and courageous. Do not be afraid; do not be discouraged, for the Lord your God will be with you wherever you go.*

"What do you think, Audrey?"

Nathanial's question snapped her to attention. "I'm sorry?"

He held out his hand. She closed the gap between them, slipping her hand into his.

"I want to know what you think of the plan," he said.

His dark eyes searched her face. She flushed as she realized she had no idea what they'd decided. That was so unlike her. Usually she had to be in control, the one calling the shots. But she was letting Nathanial take the lead. She was putting her trust and her life into his hands. "Can you run the plan by me again?"

"I approach the cottage from the front. Make sure they see me coming. I will distract whoever's inside so that you, Blake, Sheriff Crump and the deputies can enter through the back and rescue your mother."

Dread clamped a steely hand around her throat. "You'll be vulnerable to an attack."

"Yes. Can't be helped." He squeezed her hand. "This is happening because of me. I need to end this."

"No. I won't allow you to walk directly into the line of fire," she said in a strangled voice. She felt as if her throat were collapsing on itself.

"The priority is your mother." He tucked a strand of her hair behind her ear, his touch gentle and electric. "I'll do whatever it takes."

He was so generous and brave. His courage gave her the motivation she needed to pull herself together. She squared her shoulders with determination. "You're not going in alone. I'll have your back, while Uncle David and Blake rescue Mom."

"Thank you. But—"

She placed her finger firmly against his lips. "No *but*."

His gaze softened and filled with something that made her heart pound and her blood race.

Despite the grim circumstances and the fear crowding her, Audrey realized how deeply she'd come to care for this man as she found strength in his dark gaze.

"Okay, now that that is settled," David said. "Agent Fallon and I will organize the troops. Audrey, take Officer Longhorn to the equipment room for a flak vest."

"Yes, sir." Keeping hold of Nathanial's hand, she led him to the back of the station, where they kept extra equipment.

They entered, but before she could reach for a flak vest, Nathanial tugged her close. The room was cold, but pressed up against Nathanial, she felt warmed from the inside out.

He cupped her cheek. "Whatever happens today, I want you to know that I—"

Flutters of excitement made her hold her breath. "You?"

"Am thoroughly, totally in love with you," he said. Then he kissed her.

Shock from his words vied with the magnificent sensation of his mouth moving over hers, chasing away the gnawing little voice that warned her not to believe it. Hadn't she made the mistake before of buying into a charming man's declaration?

But this was Nathanial. And, oh, his kiss made her knees weak. He was a good man. An honorable man.

A man willing to sacrifice his life for her mother's safe return.

A declaration born out of desperation and fear couldn't be trusted. She broke the kiss and stepped back. Her head was reeling, her heart groaning with longing and need. But she had to be smart.

"You are not going to die today. I forbid it. And when this is over, then…" Then what? She didn't know. Couldn't see beyond the immediate need to rescue her mother.

She grabbed a flak vest from the rack and shoved it into his chest. "Put this on. I'll get you a weapon."

"I have Drew's Glock still," he said as he donned the vest, his expression unreadable.

"Good." She opened a cabinet and took out a bolt-action Remington 700 sniper rifle used by police departments all across the United States. She grabbed a box of ammo.

Catching the incredulous expression on Nathanial's face, she arched an eyebrow. "What? You're not the only one who can do overwatch."

He barked out a laugh. "You are a treasure, Deputy Audrey Martin."

"And don't you forget it." She walked out with the rifle tucked under her arm.

Nathanial held up his hands as he approached the front of the Martin cottage. He'd parked Blake's SUV at the end of the driveway. The sound of the nearby ocean drowned out the thrumming of blood in his ears. The place looked like something right out of a Thomas Kinkade painting.

A cobblestone path led to a large wooden door, where a green wreath sporting a red bow hung in welcome. The eaves were dusted white, and little colorful Christmas lights peeked through, reminding him that tomorrow was Christmas Eve. A fully trimmed tree with lush boughs dominated the front window and kept him from seeing inside.

But that didn't mean those inside couldn't see him. He prayed they couldn't see Audrey. Even though he couldn't see Audrey's perch, he could feel her gaze as surely as if she were standing beside him. She had his back. She'd had his back from the moment he'd washed ashore on the beach.

He stopped at the foot of three stone steps. "I'm here. Let Dr. Martin go."

The front door opened. A man hung back in the shadows of the darkened house. "We'll let her go when we're ready. Come in."

The heavily accented voice wasn't Chase's. Kosloff? Would he be bold enough to do his own dirty work? Nathanial couldn't make out the man's face—he stayed just out of the light enough to keep hidden.

"What assurances do I have that you won't kill her?" Nathanial called back.

The tip of a rifle poked out of the door. "You don't."

"I'm not coming in until I know Dr. Martin is unharmed," he said, bracing himself. It would be too easy for the man in the doorway to put a bullet between Nathanial's eyes. But then the shooter would also find himself on the receiving end of Audrey's bullet.

The man disappeared. When he returned to the door, he held Dr. Martin by his beefy hand. A ski mask covered his face, which was a good sign. If Dr. Martin couldn't identify him, there was no reason to kill her.

Nathanial turned his attention to Dr. Martin. She had a gag over her mouth. She wore her hospital lab coat, and her wide-eyed gaze locked with his. He saw her terror, but he also saw her strength. She was afraid, but she wasn't cowering. She was, after all, Audrey's mother, and Audrey had learned to be strong from the woman who'd raised her. "It's going to be okay," Nathanial assured her.

The man jerked her back into the house. "Now you come in."

"Sure." Nathanial stepped onto the first stair. "Where's Chase?"

"Stop stalling," the man yelled. "Get in here."

A loud bang from the back of the house distracted the man at the door. He turned toward the sound. Nathanial vaulted up the stairs and tackled the guy, taking him down to the cherry hardwood floor in a heap. Nathanial scrambled for dominance and landed a well-placed punch to the man's jaw, knocking him out.

Dr. Martin crouched down behind the couch as Blake,

Sheriff Crump and Deputy Paulson came into the living room with another masked man with hands cuffed in tow.

The sheriff hurried to Dr. Martin's side and quickly released the gag from over her mouth and the rope binding her hands together. She hugged her uncle.

"We found this one in the kitchen," Blake said as he pushed the man to his knees. Gripping the edge of his ski mask, Blake ripped off the mask. Nathanial didn't recognize the guy. "Not Chase."

Focusing on the unconscious man, Nathanial stripped him of the mask. "Not him, either." Blake handed Nathanial a set of zip ties to cuff the man's hands together.

"I'll let Audrey know to come in." The sheriff pulled out his phone and stepped to the front window next to the Christmas tree.

Nathanial could only imagine the relief Audrey would feel learning her mother was safe. He wanted to go to her. He still had trouble believing he'd told her he loved her. The admission had bubbled up without forethought. But he didn't regret it.

That she hadn't expressed any similar sentiment stung. Though he couldn't fault her. There would be time enough later to discover if she felt the same. And if she didn't... he didn't want to think about how lonely and unfulfilling his life would be without her in it.

"Dr. Martin," Blake said. "Can you tell us what happened?"

"I was leaving the hospital when a man approached me," she said. "He had a badge and said he was here to protect me. He drove me home. Then he surprised the stuffing out of me when he tied me up and locked me in the bedroom so I'd be out of the way."

"Where did he go?" Nathanial asked.

She shook her head. "I don't know. It's been hours since

I've seen anyone until that one came in and brought me to the door."

Blake addressed the man on his knees. "Where's your boss?"

The guy stayed stubbornly silent.

"What was the plan?" Blake asked. "Were you to kill Officer Longhorn?"

The suspect's gaze flicked to Nathanial then away. Nathanial took that as a yes. Disappointment filled him. This wasn't over, but at least Dr. Martin was safe.

"That's odd," the sheriff said as he turned from the window. "She's not picking up."

Dread crept up the back of Nathanial's spine. That was the one thing about overwatch—you had everyone else's back, but no one had yours.

He raced from the house, tore down the drive and scrambled up the hill that faced the cottage and the ocean. The place where he'd left Audrey was empty save for her rifle and flak vest. Eerily similar to what Drew had said Nathanial's disappearance had looked like. Terror clawed through him with razor-sharp talons.

He had to get to the ocean before they could throw her in as they had him.

SIXTEEN

Awareness came in spurts of sensation. Cold seeped through Audrey's clothes. Light filtered through her silted eyes and stung her retinas. The roar of the ocean in her ears. The salty taste of brine filled her mouth and nose. The gentle rocking of a boat buffeted by waves made her stomach roil. Her head throbbed, and her arms were pulled back in an awkward position and bound at the wrists by a thin rope.

Anger erupted within her chest, heating her skin and her mind. *Oh, no, you didn't just kidnap me!*

She held herself still, taking stock, assessing the situation. She needed to be smart, wait for an opportunity to escape. But first she had to know what she was dealing with. And whom.

After a recon of the area above her mom's cottage to make sure it was safe, she'd taken a position perched in the snow-covered V of a large paper birch tree that stood less than fifty yards from the cottage. She'd watched through the Nikon scope attached to her Remington rifle as Nathanial walked up the path leading to her mother's front door. There had been a noise behind her, just a whisper of sound. Expecting to see one of the white-tailed deer that were in abundance in Maine, she'd glanced over her shoul-

der at the exact moment that she'd been struck in the head
with the butt of a rifle.

Just as Nathanial had been when he'd been taken from
the rooftop in New Brunswick. Though in her case, she
thankfully had her memories. A blessing, to be sure.

But why take her? They could have killed her or left
her there unconscious. The answer washed over her with
a sickening certainty.

To punish Nathanial. To use her as leverage against
him. Chase had worked with Nathanial and for some reason must hold some ill will against him.

Well, little did her captors realize they'd messed with
the wrong woman.

Slowly she shifted, hoping for a better view of her sur-
roundings. The boat was the open picnic style of a local
boat maker. She recognized the company logo on the floorboard. It wasn't a fast boat, nor one meant for choppy waters, which led her to believe whoever had her wasn't from
Down East and had no idea how dangerous taking the
small day cruiser into the winter ocean would be.

No doubt they planned to take her out to sea and dump
her overboard the way they had Nathanial. She wasn't sure
if her captors were cowards, unwilling to actually do the
killing, or if they took joy from cruelty.

A foot appeared in her line of sight. Droplets of blood
splattered the top and sides of the heavy black boot.

She ground her teeth together. But whose blood?

"Drop him over there," a man said. The timbre of his
voice struck a chord within her. She'd heard it before. It
wasn't Chase's. But it was American.

Oh, no. *Please, Lord, don't let them have taken Nathanial, too.*

The thud of a body hitting the floorboard jolted through
her but was outside her field of vision. Unless she wanted

to give away that she was conscious, she couldn't move to see who lay there.

"We've got a problem," another man stated. One of Kosloff's thugs, if the accent was any indication. "Ivan and Sven were captured."

"I should've known," the first man said. "Kosloff will not be pleased. But now that we have Longhorn's girlfriend, he'll come to us, and then we can finally get rid of him."

Audrey's stomach churned. She was correct. They planned to use her to bait Nathanial into a trap.

But if it wasn't Nathanial they'd dragged aboard, then who?

The boat's motor revved as they began to move.

"Halt! Sheriff's department!" Deputy Harrison yelled.

"Stop!" shouted a familiar voice. Nathanial!

Gunfire erupted over her head. She sent up a plea that God would keep those onshore safe. *Keep Nathanial safe*, she prayed.

Nathanial watched with helpless frustration as the boat taking Audrey away raced through the churning waves until it was a tiny speck. He held Drew's Glock in his hand, but he hadn't fired. He'd been too afraid of hitting Audrey, who had been lying unconscious on the deck. The sight made his blood run cold. There were no other boats on the private dock. Short of jumping in the ocean and swimming, there was nothing he could do.

He'd failed her. He went to his knees on the wet, slick dock. "Please, dear God. Don't let them hurt her."

Blake tucked his weapon into his holster. "We'll get her back. Sheriff Crump is on the line with the coast guard now."

The older man was hurrying back toward the cottage with his phone clutched to his ear.

"What if they dump her overboard?" Nathanial said. He couldn't take it if she died because of him. He never should have let her take overwatch. He shouldn't have let her come anywhere near the danger. He shook his head, knowing there'd been no way he could have stopped her. She was a brave, strong and stubborn woman who had proved over and over again that she was capable and good at her job.

And he couldn't fault her for letting someone get the drop on her. Not when the same thing had happened to him.

Blake held out his hand. "Come on. We need to figure out what these guys in the cottage know."

Nathanial grasped his friend's hand and rose to his feet. They hurried back to the house, where Deputy Paulson was standing guard over the two thugs. The sheriff was with Dr. Martin in the kitchen, explaining the situation. Nathanial's heart bled for her. She'd endured her own kidnapping and now her daughter had been taken. None of this would have happened had he not been beached on the sand like a whale.

Blake bent down so he was eye level with one of the men. "Listen carefully. I'm only going to offer this once. If you tell me where your boss's base of operation is now, I'll talk to the prosecutor about not deporting you. Because we both know you'll fare better in the US prison system than in your home country."

Nathanial crossed his arms over his chest, tucking his hands under his arms to keep from reaching out and pummeling the two goons until they gave up the information they needed to find Audrey.

"You talk, we're dead," the other thug said.

"Sven, we'll have a better chance of not being dead if they get Kosloff," the other goon argued.

"Not if we end up in the same prison," Sven said.

Antsy with the need to do something, Nathanial stepped closer. "We'll make sure you're protected." The offer grated on his nerves but he'd do, give, offer, anything to find Audrey.

"He has a warehouse on Moose Island." The thug in front of Blake gave him directions to Kosloff's hideout.

"Ivan!" His buddy groaned then pinned Nathanial with pleading eyes. "You'll protect us? Kosloff is not someone you want to cross."

"Tell me the name of the American who's working with Kosloff," Nathanial demanded.

The two men glanced at each other. "Which one?"

"The one in law enforcement," Blake specified.

Ivan shrugged. "Kosloff has many officers working for him in many countries. We don't know names. It's better that way."

Nathanial's jaw ached from the force with which he clenched it. "Call Director Moore. We need everyone on this."

Blake rose. "We'll call from the car. The sheriff and his men can handle these two."

Before Nathanial stepped out of the cottage, Dr. Martin stopped him with a hand on his arm.

"Please, find my daughter and bring her home safely," she asked him. Her blue eyes, so like Audrey's, dug at him.

He covered her hand with his own. "I wil!."

Even if he died trying.

The boat halted, the engine dying with a gurgle. Audrey tensed. Where were they? She'd tried calculating the distance in her mind, but chills had set in, distracting her. Was this the moment when her captors would throw her overboard? No. She remembered what the man in charge had said. They were going to use her to lure Nathanial into a death trap.

"Bring them." The command came from the American.

Rough hands grabbed at her. She couldn't afford to pretend any longer. She came to struggling. Kicking with her bound legs and twisting, turning.

A large hand slapped her across the face. "Stop it. Or I'll do worse."

She opened her eyes fully and met the angry gaze of a big and burly man with a mean expression on an otherwise bland face. He lifted her from the floor of the boat and flung her over his massive shoulder.

Mortified by the undignified position, she levered herself as high as she could and took stock of the location. The boat had docked at a lone pier. She could see Calico Bay in the distance. They had to be on Moose Island. Relief washed through her. She knew this place.

The lug carrying her set her unceremoniously on the hard concrete floor of a large warehouse, propped up against the south-facing wall. High windows let in light but blocked the view in and out of the building. Another thug dragged the other captive, still unconscious, across the floor and left him in a heap next to her.

Rage simmered low in her belly as she watched the men move to take a standing position along bench tables to clean their weapons. The scent of gun oil mingled with the dank smell of the warehouse. She had to find a way out of here. A way to warn Nathanial to not come for her, that he'd be walking into a trap. The roll-up door they'd come in through closed with a loud grating sound that stroked the hairs at the back of her neck to attention.

A staircase at one end of the warehouse led to an office. The lights were on, and she could see the silhouettes of several men through the closed window shade. Kosloff and his high-ranking minions. The only other exit was a side door that she prayed led to the outside. She worked the rope around her wrists, desperate to loosen its hold on her. The skin around her wrists burned, but she continued on.

The heap of a man lying on the ground beside her groaned. The back of his blond head was matted with blood. He lay facing away from her, so she'd yet to identify him. His hands and feet were bound like hers were.

"Hey," she whispered, hoping the man would come to so he could help her untie the cord around her wrists. "Wake up."

She shifted so she could push at him with her feet. "Come on."

He moaned as he flipped to his back, revealing his face.

Shocked rippled through her. "Chase!"

How could this be? He'd been the one to call her, threatening her mother's life if she didn't bring Nathanial to him. Had Kosloff turned on the ATF agent?

Chase's eyes fluttered open. For a moment he lay still, then his body jerked as he tried to rise but the binding holding his hands and feet together prevented him from doing more than flopping about like a fish on a hook.

"Stop," Audrey commanded in a harsh whisper, afraid he'd pull his arms out of their sockets, and then he'd be of no use to her.

He froze. His gaze zeroed on her. "What happened? Where are we?"

Darting a glance at their jailers to make sure they hadn't drawn anyone's attention, she hissed, "Shh. Not so loud."

Too late. One man left his place and came to stand over her. It was the same lug who'd carried her inside like a sack of potatoes. She bared her teeth at him with a growl of rage and frustration.

He hunkered down in front of her. His breath smelled

worse than rotten fish on a hot summer day. "You're a little wildcat. We could have some fun."

He dared to skim his knuckles down her cheek. She pressed into his touch as if seeking his caress before jerking her head toward his fingers and chomping down hard on his pinkie.

He let out a yowl of pain and fell back on his behind. "Ow. She bit me."

"Try that again and I'll bite it clean off," she ground out, which his buddies found hilarious. They barked out laughter at the goon's expense.

He raised a hand to hit her.

"No!" Chase shouted and swung his legs in front of Audrey. Though she appreciated his attempt to stave off the blow, she braced herself.

The thug hesitated.

Audrey leveled her gaze on him in challenge. "You think your boss will be okay with you abusing me?"

He let out a disgusted snarl and jumped to his feet. Audrey let out a relieved breath as the lug stalked back to his weapon.

Chase shimmied to the wall and used it as leverage to bring himself to a sitting position. "Your mother?"

"Safe." Audrey narrowed her gaze on him. "You're working with Kosloff? How could you betray Nathanial like that?"

"No. I'm not. Absolutely not," he insisted in a harsh tone. "They forced me to make that call. He threatened to hurt my wife and daughter."

Her heart thumped. "We have to escape before Nathanial and the others walk into a trap."

Chase's gaze lifted to the office. "Kosloff and Wellborn are in there."

Surprised, she stared at him. "Wellborn? Luke?" An

image of the baby-faced agent rose in her mind. He'd seemed so sincere when she'd met him. "The border patrol agent is the one working with Kosloff? The one who betrayed Nathanial?"

"Yes." The bitter tone lacing Chase's voice made her shiver. "He's the one responsible for the deaths of my men and the one who's been trying to kill Nathanial."

A fresh wave of fury infused her, heating her blood. "We need to untie these ropes."

He shifted so he was semisideways. "Put your shoulder against mine so they can't see what we're up to."

She maneuvered into position. Pressing close to him so he could work at the knot in the rope. She kept her gaze on the men, barely daring to take a breath, and sent up a prayer that none of the thugs would notice what they were doing. The seconds ticked by until she felt the rope loosen enough that she could slip a hand out.

"My turn," she said beneath her breath and began working the cord binding Chase's wrists.

The small side door banged open, and one of Kosloff's men rushed inside. "They're here," he announced before racing to the office with his proclamation.

Audrey's stomach dropped. She plucked at the rope around Chase's wrists with renewed vigor. They had to get their hands on some weapons.

Four men filed out of the upstairs office. Audrey recognized Luke and two of the thugs. They'd been on the boat with them. But the fourth man she'd only seen in photos. Kosloff. He wore an expensive-looking suit beneath a wool trench coat and sported a furry Ushanka hat, the traditional headwear of Russia.

"Bring me the woman." Kosloff's guttural voice carried across the warehouse.

Ack. She wasn't done with Chase's rope.

"Leave it," Chase said. "Save yourself."

She had every intention of saving them all.

Giving up on Chase's cord, she pressed her back to the wall to hide the fact that her hands were free. A different thug hurried over, grabbed her by the biceps and forced her to her feet. He had the strap of a semiautomatic slung over his shoulder. The weapon bumped into her as he pushed her toward his boss.

"Kosloff, we have the place surrounded." Blake's deep voice sounded through the warehouse walls. "Come out with your hands up."

Kosloff snickered. "Not likely." He peered at Audrey. "Too bad you must die. I could use an amazon like you in my stable."

Audrey's lip curled in a sneer. Her hands fisted with the need to disabuse him of that thought. But she held herself still. The timing wasn't right yet for her to make a move.

Noise on the roof sent her pulse careening. Her body tensed. The sound of glass breaking as men swung through the windows was the distraction she needed. She whirled on the goon holding her arm. Using the side of her hand, she chopped into his throat. He doubled over. She slipped the strap off his shoulder and gripped the semiautomatic in her hands. Two thugs stepped in front of Kosloff, blocking her aim.

A team of men dropped into the warehouse with weapons drawn. Kosloff's men formed a circle with Audrey and Kosloff in the middle. They were at a standoff.

Luke held up his hands. "Whoa! Everyone take a breath. No one wants to die today."

Nathanial separated from the others. He had Audrey's Remington aimed at Luke's chest. "Wellborn!" The hurt in his voice made Audrey wince. "You're the traitor? Why?"

Luke shrugged. "I needed the money. Tell your men to lower their weapons or we all die."

"I don't think so." Nathanial pushed his way through the men to Audrey's side. "You're surrounded. Outmanned and outgunned."

Luke smirked. "You don't think I know your moves?" He made a sweeping motion with his hand. "These are only the men you can see. There are many more waiting to mobilize."

Audrey couldn't discern if Luke was bluffing.

"Enough of this," Kosloff said. "Kill them all and be done with it. I want to get home in time for Christmas Eve dinner."

Tension rippled through Audrey as a barrage of gunfire erupted around her. Kosloff and Luke ran toward the exit, followed by the two protective goons. She fired, hitting one thug in the leg. He went down. The other thug pivoted and turned the barrel of his weapon toward her.

"Audrey, look out!" Nathanial cried. He shoved her hard as the goon pulled the trigger.

Nathanial jerked and fell unconscious at Audrey's feet.

"No!" Audrey's scream bounced off the concrete floor. She sank to her knees and cradled him in her arms. His head bled from the bullet. "No, please don't leave me."

The roller door opened, and a swarm of additional federal agents stormed in and quickly subdued the few remaining thugs. But all Audrey could concentrate on was the man in her arms. The man she loved with her whole being.

"Please, Lord, let him live."

Nathanial awoke to the beeping of monitors and the white stucco ceiling of the Calico Bay hospital. A sense of déjà vu hit him with the force of a nor'easter. Only this time there was no void where his memories should have been. His memories were intact.

Including everything that had happened in the past week.

It all came rushing to the forefront of his mind. Being hit from behind while on overwatch. Being dragged onto a boat and seeing Luke Wellborn's familiar face. The icy shock of the ocean water when Luke and another goon had dumped him overboard. Then the beautiful woman who'd rescued him on the beach.

Audrey!

He had to know she was safe. He grappled with the bed to find the nurse's call button. Frantic with worry, he depressed the button repeatedly.

When Kosloff's thug had put her in his sights, Nathanial had reacted. He'd pushed her aside, taking the hit himself. That he wasn't dead was a blessing. He didn't know why God had spared him, but he sent up a grateful prayer of praise.

The door opened. Dr. Martin hurried in. "Are you in pain?"

"No." He gripped the bed railing. "Audrey? Is she okay?"

Dr. Martin's expression softened as she took his vitals. "She's outside with the others. I'll let them know you're awake."

He lay back with relief and became aware of the throbbing in his head. Worse than it was before. "I was shot."

She made a noise very reminiscent of one her daughter had made when he'd stated the obvious and she wrote on his chart. "The bullet grazed your forehead. You most likely have another concussion. I don't recommend any more."

"My memories came back," he told her.

"That's good news. It's been known to happen after a head contusion." She set the chart aside and pinned him with a sober look. "What are your intentions with my daughter?"

Taken aback by the blunt question, he blurted, "I'm afraid of love. Afraid of the hurt that can come with it."

"So is she," Dr. Martin said. "But the greatest blessings lie beyond your greatest fears."

He absorbed her wise words, thinking that was something his own mother would say. He searched his heart. He loved Audrey, but was he willing to risk it all without knowing how she felt about him? Especially now that his life was no longer in danger and she was no longer obligated to protect him?

The past pain of losing his child and the sting of Laurie's rejection lay on his heart. Though the wounds were not gone, they were healed. He'd always mourn the loss of the baby, but Laurie had been right not to marry him. He could see that now.

Their love had been young and flawed.

He thought of all the years he'd held on to his grief and pain as a shield from feeling anything like that again. But it took losing his memories and a beautiful deputy sheriff to make him see that the past shouldn't dictate his future.

A future he wanted to share with Audrey, if she'd have him.

He met Dr. Martin's gaze and spoke with earnestness. "I love your daughter and want to spend the rest of my life with her."

The older woman's eyes lit up. "I'm glad to hear it." She turned and nearly danced from the room.

A few moments later, Audrey came in, followed by Blake, Drew and Sami. Nathanial only had eyes for the uniformed deputy who stopped at the foot of the bed. Her gaze caressed him, and he wished they were alone so he could explore that look.

"Hey," Blake said, drawing his attention. "You scared us a second time."

Nathanial gave him a lopsided grin. "Well, apparently the second time is a charm, because my memories have returned. All of them."

"That's great," Sami exclaimed.

Drew gave him the thumbs-up sign. "Most excellent."

"I thought the saying was three times is a charm," Blake retorted with a grin.

"Please, God, don't let there be a third time," Nathanial quipped.

"That's great, Nathanial," Audrey said softly.

Blake withdrew a box from inside his coat. "I thought you might want this back."

Nathanial lifted his eyebrows. Blake opened the lid to reveal a lethal-looking steel knife. "My Becker Necker. Thanks, dude."

Blake set it on the eating tray by the bed. "Your government wants you back ASAP. And the director wants to debrief us all as well. It doesn't look good for one of our own to be an accomplice with Kosloff."

"Right. How's Chase?" Nathanial asked. His mind still reeled with the knowledge that Luke had betrayed them. For money. The root of all evil, or so they said.

"He's fine. Livid, as we all are," Drew said.

A moment of silence pervaded the room.

"We should let Audrey and Nathanial have a moment alone," Sami said, her keen gaze bouncing between them.

"That's subtle." Her husband laughed. "We'll check with Dr. Martin to see when she'll release you."

They filed out of the room. Audrey remained at the end

of the bed. An awkward tension filled the space between them. He held out his hand.

She rounded the bed and twined her fingers through his. "I was so afraid I'd lost you."

Though he didn't like that she'd been scared, he couldn't keep a dopey grin from forming. "Lose me? Never."

"You remembered why you never allowed yourself to fall in love," she said. "Is that still the case?"

"No. The past is over."

Her big blue eyes were so full of love that he felt his own eyes welling up. Whoa. He wasn't a crier. "I love you, Audrey." He rushed the words out before he was too choked up to speak.

"When you said that before, I thought it was only because you thought you were going to die," she stated in a soft, uncertain tone.

"I said it because it's true."

"I know." She brought his hand to her mouth and kissed his knuckles. "I love you, too," she murmured against his skin.

His heart skipped a beat. "Come again?"

She lowered his hand, squared her shoulders and lifted her chin. His warrior bracing for battle. "For too long I've let fear keep me from accepting that anyone could love me for me."

He held up his other hand. "I do."

She gave a small laugh. "I know."

"A wise woman recently told me that our greatest blessings lie beyond our greatest fears." He squeezed her hand. "I want to be your greatest blessing."

She beamed at him. "I love you."

His heart soared with joy. But then crashed to the ground. "I have to go back to Canada."

"Not until after Christmas," she stated. "Mom won't sign off on letting you travel until next week."

"I like the sound of that, but…" He didn't want to think about leaving her.

"But we'll tackle the future after Christmas. I'm in," she said. "Whatever may come, wherever we end up, as long as we're together, I'm good."

Tears slipped down his cheeks. "Give me a kiss before I start blubbering like a baby."

She leaned in to place her lips against his in a kiss that made the world fade away.

EPILOGUE

One year later

The Christmas tree twinkled in the window of the cottage by the sea. Audrey stepped back after putting on the last decoration. "It's perfect."

"Not quite," her husband said as he slipped an arm around her waist and held out a box wrapped in red paper and gold ribbon.

"Nathanial, Christmas isn't for a few more weeks," she exclaimed but snatched the pretty box from his hands anyway.

He laughed and kissed the side of her neck. "I don't want to wait."

His impatience was one of his most endearing and annoying qualities. With a grin, she sank down on the plush rug covering the hardwood floor. He sat beside her. His eagerness for her to open the gift was so cute she sighed with contentment. She had everything in life she could want. A wonderful husband, a home and a community to protect.

After their summer wedding, her mother had gifted them with the cottage, saying a young couple needed space to grow. The obvious hint at providing grandchildren wasn't lost on Audrey. Mom had moved into Audrey's studio in town and was dating the bank manager.

Nathanial had convinced the powers that be of the need for an IBETs presence Down East. Being married to a US citizen allowed him to live in Calico Bay. And when he had to leave on a mission, Bangor airport was only a few hours away.

She slipped the knot out of the ribbon and laid the gold material to the side.

Nathanial groaned. "You're torturing me on purpose."

She giggled then ripped through the paper to reveal a white box. Jewelry? She glanced at the marquise-cut diamond on her finger. That was all the decoration she needed. She opened the box. Nestled against cotton batting was a beautiful, shiny ornament in the shape of a star.

With a gasp, she lifted it up to catch the light and turned stunned eyes to the man she loved. "It's lovely."

He grinned, his dark eyes shining bright. "You don't remember, do you?"

Searching her brain and coming up empty, she said, "Can I claim amnesia?"

"Hey!" He laughed and shook his head. "What were the first words I said to you?"

She was mentally transported to that day on the beach when she'd found him lying on the sand. "'Betrayed.'"

"No, not that. The other thing."

She looked at him blankly.

"When I woke up in the hospital," he prompted.

The heat of a blush swept up her cheeks. "You said I looked like a Christmas ornament. Shiny. Pretty." Now the gift made sense. She hugged it to her chest.

He leaned in to kiss her. "Merry Christmas, my shiny, pretty wife."

* * * * *

If you enjoyed IDENTITY UNKNOWN,
look for the other books in the
NORTHERN BORDER PATROL *series:*

DANGER AT THE BORDER
JOINT INVESTIGATION
MURDER UNDER THE MISTLETOE
RANSOM.

Dear Reader,

Thank you for joining me in the last installment of the Northern Border Patrol series. It was time to give Canadian officer Nathanial Longhorn his own book, and pairing him strong and independent Deputy Sheriff Audrey Martin seemed like the perfect match.

Giving Nathanial amnesia was such fun. It was a delight to have him learning about himself as he fell in love with Audrey. They both had painful issues from their past to overcome in order to have their happy ending. Audrey's mother shared a piece of wisdom with Nathanial—our greatest blessings lie beyond our greatest fears. Do you believe that?

I do. Sometimes in life we have to move past our fear in order to find the blessing. I pray you will find your blessing this holiday season.

Keep watch for a new K-9 continuity series in 2017. Check out my webpage at terrireed.com and sign up for my newsletter for updates on my new releases.

Merry Christmas and happy New Year!

Blessings,